it started with a dare

# it started with a dare

### Lindsay Faith Rech

Houghton Mifflin Harcourt
Boston New York 2010

All rights reserved. Published in the United States by Graphia,
an imprint of Houghton Mifflin Harcourt Publishing Company.

For information about permission to reproduce selections from this book,
write to Permissions, Houghton Mifflin Harcourt Publishing Company,
215 Park Avenue South, New York, New York 10003.

Graphia and the Graphia logo are registered trademarks of
Houghton Mifflin Harcourt Publishing Company.

www.hmhbooks.com

The text of this book is set in Bembo.
Book design by Susanna Vagt.

Library of Congress Cataloging-in-Publication Data
Rech, Lindsay Faith, 1978–
It started with a dare / Lindsay Faith Rech.
p. cm.
Summary: When fifteen-year-old honors student Cynthia Gene Silverman
moves to a new school, she decides to reinvent herself as a reckless daredevil in
order to be accepted by the popular clique.
ISBN 978-0-547-23558-5 (pbk. original : alk. paper) [1. Cliques (Sociology)—
Fiction. 2. Individuality—Fiction. 3. Conduct of life—Fiction. 4. High
schools—Fiction. 5. Schools—Fiction. 6. Identity—Fiction.] I. Title.
PZ7.R2383It 2010
[Fic]—dc22
2009050014

Manufactured in the United States of America
DOM 10 9 8 7 6 5 4 3 2 1

4500241969

To Scott for more than a decade of laughter
and unwavering support; for the life coaching and
friendship; and for giving me the most beautiful gift
I've ever known—our daughter, Jayla. Thanks for
everything, Erdie. We did it!

# *one* getting in

Every school has one. At my last school, it was Gina DiMarco, but she never cared much for me. Okay, fine, if you want to be a total stickler about it, she never even knew I existed. I guess it's like that at most schools. The "It" girl only pays attention to the worthy ones, the inner circle, the worshipful flock who kneel at her feet, feeding off her every word like a pack of anorexic poodles. The rest of us are merely space fillers, extras in a tragically boring movie unimaginatively entitled "High School." But if that's true, then *what,* I ask you, is this latest queen bee—the Gina DiMarco of Beaubridge High—doing talking to an invisible nobody like me? And smack dab in the middle of the cafeteria no less? Everyone knows that what happens in the cafeteria never *stays* in the cafeteria. Is she looking to lose her tiara?

"Hey, you're new here, right?" she asks. *She,* of course,

being the reigning duchess of teen suburbia—the impossibly stunning Alona Spelton. It's true I've barely been here five hours, but how long does it take to spot royalty? (Even if my radar were out of batteries, the mass of drooling subjects crumbling in her wake as she sashayed through the halls this morning was sort of a dead giveaway.) She slips into a seat at my otherwise empty table and smiles. "I think you're in my homeroom."

Let's face it, the first day at a new school's never exactly a raging orgasm. But try the first day at a new school in the middle of the year, when everyone's just returned from winter break and not a single bloody soul wants to be there. Including the teachers. This little visit from the acceptance fairy has definitely perked things up a bit.

"Yeah, I, um, just moved here from Philadelphia," I say, eyeing the white gold and diamond ice storm that surrounds her delicate wrist. Scratch that. This girl wouldn't let anything but platinum touch her bare skin. Me, I'm still wearing the same beat-up, old woven fabric friendship bracelet my buddy Alex gave me when we graduated middle school. But that's the difference between these kids and me. To them, being poor means only having one beach house.

"Philadelphia?" Alona asks, her vibrant blue eyes twinkling with amazement. Or maybe it's disgust. *You don't* smell *like you're from Philadelphia,* I expect her to say.

Instead, she smiles. "You know, that stunt you pulled with Ms. Luru this morning was *waaay* cool—cracking your gum in her face like that even *after* she started glaring at you to stop. I swear I thought she was going to have a conniption." *Did I do that?* Hell, who cares? If it gets me in with Alona Spelton, I'll take credit for just about any bad behavior. Except maybe arson.

"Well, it's a free country," I say, trying to sound nonchalant. "And last time I checked, cracking one's gum in homeroom was still covered under our Constitution."

Alona laughs, tossing her wavy amber tresses so that they land like a perfectly cascading waterfall over her right shoulder. Uh, is it me or did I just stumble into an Herbal Essences commercial? "Sammie! Grace!" she yells, signaling to two girls who have just left the lunch line. "Over here!"

Wait, rewind just a second. Would any of you happen to know if today's brown bag special was laced with a little something extra? Because if I'm not hallucinating, that means this totally tripped-out scenario is actually taking place! Can you stand it? My first day of school, and I'm already dining with the worthy ones? Just the inner circle and *me?* Uh . . . who else senses there's something wrong with this picture?

"So, what's your name again?" Alona asks as she opens her Styrofoam container of . . . Is that *sushi?*

"Cynthia Gene," I say, biting into my soggy PB&J, "but my friends just call me CG." Not that I have many friends. Or any. Well, except for Alex, who was always sort of more than a friend. And who was sort of more than pissed when I told him I wanted to be free to see other people after I moved. Not that Philadelphia's that far away from Beaubridge. I could be on his doorstep in forty-five minutes if I wanted to. But I'm not sure I do. I'm not sure what I want anymore. Except to be different. To be popular. I've been waiting my whole life for that.

"CG?" Alona asks, shrieking a little—you know, in that *Oh, that's so adorable, I could just choke to death* sort of way. "That is *soooo* cute!" She turns to Sammie and Grace, who have just sat down on either side of her. "How cute is that?"

"*So* cute," Sammie agrees. Sammie, which I later find out is short for Samara, is a husky-framed zombie who looks like she spends about four hours a day crisping away in a tanning bed. Her hair is a glossy (but obviously bottle-bought) jet black, and her bright red lipstick makes her look like a bleeding ox. Her brain? Seems to be dead as a doornail. Still, at least she's being nice to me, even if it *is* only to please Alona. But why would someone like Alona Spelton want anything to do with a plain, grubby city tomboy type like me?

"You know, I think our fathers work together," the Duchess says. "Your last name's Silverman, right?"

I nod. So *that's* why Miss Teenage America is being so lovey-dovey. Her father must've warned her. I watch plenty of movies—I know how these rich families operate. It's all about pleasing Daddy.

Alona smiles. "That's so crazy. My dad is your dad's boss." She turns to Sammie and Grace again. "Isn't that crazy? I mean, how crazy is that?"

"*So* crazy," Sammie agrees. She shoots me a little smile. "Like, what are the chances?"

"Oh, wait a second," Grace says to Alona. "Is this the one you were telling me about? The one whose family Klytech was going to set up in that little townhouse in the Heights?" Her voice drops a notch or two when she mentions the name of my development, probably because the Heights is best known in this community for its affordable housing. In rich-people speak, I'm about one step away from the projects.

"Grace!" Alona shrieks. Although this time, it's more of a *Shut it before we all die of mortification* shriek.

"No, it's cool," I say. "It's probably no secret from the way I'm dressed that my family doesn't have a lot of dough. If Klytech hadn't set us up in that 'little townhouse,' we'd all still be living on the streets of Filthadelphia."

Grace turns away from me, clearly embarrassed, but the awkward silence is cut short by another one of Her Highness's signature shrieks. Actually, that one may have been just an outright pity gasp.

"Were you *really* living on the streets?" she asks, her sympathetic baby blues welling up at the sheer thought. I guess this would be a really inappropriate time to bust out laughing. Especially if I'm looking to make these girls my new best friends. But it's too late—Grace has caught my eye, and I recognize something in her that seems to be lacking in my other two lunch mates. (Some might call it common sense.) It isn't long before we're both hysterical.

"What is *with* you two?" Alona asks, visibly perturbed, but like a perfectly trained debutante, she's doing her best not to show it.

Grace throws her head back in a rush of giggles, her buoyant auburn curls bouncing like a bouquet of Slinkys around her graceful neck. Next to Alona and Grace, Sammie looks like their mentally retarded charity case "friend for a day" adoptee. God, I wonder what that makes *me*.

"It's nothing," Grace tells Alona, turning to her apologetically. "It's just that I knew CG was only kidding about being homeless, that's all."

"Homelessness is a *really* serious problem," Alona says, assuming an insanely dramatic tone. "I wrote a term paper on it last semester and got a B."

"Well . . . good for you," I fumble, hoping I haven't blown it. "I wrote my last term paper on whales and—"

"Oh, geez, check out Glory Finklefuss's latest crime of fashion," Grace groans, pointing to some gawky girl in the lunch line whose giant khaki overalls could easily double as a camping tent.

"Well, I don't think her parents have much money," Alona says. "From what I heard, her whole family lives in some tiny two-bedroom shack in the Hei—" She stops short and stares at me apologetically. "Sorry."

"Hey, don't worry about it," I tell her. "My parents said if things go well for my dad with this transfer, I won't have to get that afterschool job selling crack to pay for my college tuition."

The whole table laughs, even brain-dead Sammie. And I suddenly feel . . . almost *popular.*

"I guess we've just never had a friend like you before," Alona says. She turns to Sammie and Grace, and they both nod in agreement.

"You mean a friend who didn't own ten carat's worth of diamonds by the time she turned fifteen?"

"Oh, well, Alona's *sixteen,*" Grace says. "And believe

me, her pacifier was at least *twenty* carats." She turns to the Duchess, wincing playfully. "Only kidding."

"I got my driver's license over winter break," Alona tells me proudly as she reaches out to smack Grace's arm. "We were planning to go for a ride after school. Are you in?"

Oh my God, do you have any idea what this means? I've made it! One day at Rich Bitch High and I'm already receiving exclusive invites from the cream of the crop. Ladies and gentlefriends, Ms. Cynthia Gene Silverman has finally arrived.

"Earth to CG," Grace says, waving her hand in front of my face. "Alona asked if you were in."

"Me?" I smile so hard my face hurts. "I am *so* in."

# $two$ staying in

They've always called themselves the Triple Threat. Only now that they've taken me under their wondrous wings, Alona, Sammie, and Grace have to come up with a new stage name.

"Any ideas?" Alona asks as she gazes at herself in Grace's full-length cherry wood mirror. We've just been shopping. Or more precisely, *they've* just been shopping. Not that the distinction really matters. There has never been any love lost between me and the fashion industry. I couldn't care less about the latest handbag trend or who wore what on the red carpet. As long as I'm comfortable—that's what's important. Which I guess is a good thing, since comfort is about all I can afford. Still, I don't mind tagging along while my new friends flex their credit cards. Watching them is like being a fly on the wall in some mutant alien universe: I may not understand their bizarre spending rituals, but it's still fun—and flattering—to be invited along for the ride. And the orange mocha Frappuccinos we get afterward. To be honest, I'm still getting used to the taste of those. I'd sooner just stop for a round of cherry Slurpees, but 7-Eleven is totally out of their retail orbit. And if I've learned one thing about Alona Spelton, it's that she bends over backwards for nobody. Not even the newest member of her clique.

"Hey, Lon, you look amazing in that," I say, eyeing her latest ensemble—a black stretch-denim micromini and *Whoops is this see through?* white blouse that warrants its own R rating. But then again, if you've got it, flaunt it, right? I wouldn't know. I still haven't gotten it.

Alona spins around, smiling graciously. "Aw, thanks, Ceej. You don't think it's a little . . ."

"Transparent?" Grace asks.

"Well, of course it is," Alona says playfully. "That's why I bought it."

We all giggle, and suddenly there's a knock at the door.

"Come in," Grace calls.

"Hi, girls," Grace's mom says, entering the room. Unlike my own mother, whose middle-aged pouch and "mom jeans" continue to betray her frumpy homemaker status, this more sophisticated spitting image of Grace could easily pass for her older sister. "CG!" she gushes.

"It's so good to see you again." She tells me this every time she sees me, which could only mean she's as shocked as I am that the Triple Threat has actually kept me around this long (three whole weeks, to be exact).

"Good to see you, too, Mrs. Checkov."

"Oh, Alona," she says, "I ran into your mother at the salon and she wants you to give her a buzz." She turns to leave the room. "By the way, if you're going to wear a sheer blouse, you've gotta choose a nicer bra than *that*. Gracie and I just did a major spree at Victoria's Secret, and she ended up with a couple of pieces she's either going to have to stuff with water balloons or wait a few good years to grow into. And when I say 'grow,' don't think I've ruled out giving Dr. 90210 a call!" She pauses to laugh at her own joke. "But these bras were just too cute to pass up. Why don't you try one of them on?"

*Toto, I don't think we're in Kansas anymore.*

Oblivious to the jagged death rays shooting out of her daughter's eyes, Mrs. Checkov quietly exits the room while Alona reaches into her pink leather handbag to retrieve her cell. In addition to being the only kid at Beaubridge without a string of bling around my neck or wrist, I'm also the only one without a cell phone. Or an iPod. Or a laptop. Or a trust fund. Well, make that me and Glory Finklefuss, the girl my friends were dissing at lunch a few weeks ago for wearing oversized overalls.

Glory actually lives four houses down from me in the Heights, but I generally pretend I don't know her. I mean, one false move and I could *be* Glory Finklefuss. At my old school, I practically was.

"Hey, I've got an idea for a name," I tell Sammie and Grace while Alona chats with her mother on the phone. "What about the Fabulous Four?"

*"Booooring,"* Grace says, shaking her head. "We need something edgier. Don't we, Sammie?"

"For sure," Sammie says, glancing in the mirror. She puts her hand on her stomach, sucking it in as far as it will go, then exhales deeply, deflating like a big rubber Whoopee Cushion.

"Hey, that could be a name," Grace says. "*Four* Sure."

I smile teasingly. "And you thought my suggestion needed work?"

"Uh-uh," Alona suddenly interjects, folding up her phone. "I've got it. The Four Tops."

As in that crappy oldies band my parents like to dance to at weddings?

"Oh my God, what an awesome idea!" I rave. Hey, come on, I know how to brownnose with the best of 'em. "How'd you come up with that one?"

"Well . . ." Alona says, plopping down onto Grace's white satin comforter with an exaggerated air of intelligence. "Let's not kid ourselves. We all know we're the top girls at Beaubridge High, right? The ones everyone wants to be. And now there's four of us." She turns to me and beams. "So why not just tell it like it is, loud and proud?"

Holy Frappuccino, I am officially one of them! Me, with my freckled "baby face," lifeless hair, and discount clothes. Of course, I'll have to change. I mean, in order to *stay* in, I'll have to start working overtime. Then again, nobody ever said life at the top was easy.

"So, what did your mom want?" Grace asks.

"Oh." Alona rolls her eyes. "Guess who's coming home for a visit this weekend?"

"Shut *up!*" Grace gushes as if what she really wants to say is *If I stick a quarter up your butt, will you go on talking about this forever and ever?* She turns to Sammie. "Looks like we're due for another sleepover at Alona's house."

"What?" I ask. "I don't get it."

"That's because you've never met Jordan Spelton," Grace tells me. "One look at him and you'll know why none of us are interested in high school boys anymore."

"Speak for yourself," Alona says. "You are talking about my *brother,* for heaven's sake."

"Oh, come on, you know you want him," Grace teases.

"You're psycho," Alona tells her. Then, she unbuttons her blouse, flinging it behind her onto Grace's bed.

"Come on, lead me to your glorious bra collection." I turn away, faced with that age-old dilemma of where to look, which doesn't seem to be a problem for Sammie. Out of the corner of my eye, I catch her gawking at Alona's naked torso.

"Sammie, close your mouth!" Grace commands as if the husky brunette is some kind of unruly German shepherd.

"Sorry, it's just that . . . How come mine don't look like that?"

"Because Alona's perfect," Grace tells her, and I wonder if I'm the only one who is able to detect the sarcasm in her voice. "Isn't that right, Lonnie?"

"Oh, don't be crazy," Alona says modestly. "You know I just had two cavities filled last week."

*Whoa, where's Dr. 90210 when you* really *need him?*

"And I'll let you in on a secret, Sammie," Alona continues. "When I was little, I was pigeon-toed. I had to wear corrective shoes for an entire year. I mean, you couldn't tell or anything, but I knew. And that's a really hard thing for a three-year-old to go through."

"I'll bet," Sammie commiserates.

"So, CG," Alona says. "What do you say? Are you in for a sleepover at my house this weekend?"

I look up to see Her Majesty standing there in a black leather bustier that laces up the front. Grace's mother actually *bought* her that thing? Let's face it, if I'm gonna make it with these girls, I'm gonna have to start being as bold and outrageous as they are. And if money won't allow me to dress the part, I'll just have to come up with some other way to show them how wild I can be. Like, say, this weekend at the first official Four Tops sleepover.

"Of course I'm in," I say. "I'll bring the party games."

"Party games?" Grace looks confused. "We're in tenth grade, not kindergarten. I think we're a little bit past Pin the Tail on the Donkey."

"Well, obviously," I say, fumbling for a good idea. Any idea that will raise my cool quotient. Make them feed off *my* every word like a pack of anorexic poodles. "Have you ever played Truth or Dare?"

Alona rolls her eyes. "Sweetie, *everybody* has played Truth or Dare."

I smile cunningly. "Not the way I play it."

"Ooh!" Grace squeals. "Sounds dangerous."

"And we all love a little danger now and then, don't we, girls?" Alona asks.

Grace and Sammie nod, and I feel my mouth turn to paste, knowing all I have to do is reinvent the wheel by this weekend and no one will discover I just lied my crazy, pathetic ass off to score the kind of brownie points no amount of money can buy.

# three truth?

"Okay," I begin. "So, here are the rules . . ."

It's Friday night—the night of our big sleepover—
and I've spent all week trying to turn Truth or Dare
into a game that transcends secret-spilling and grade
school challenges. Something not for the faint of heart.
A game that will truly shock their senses and show them
that CG Silverman is more than just some average
schmo from Philly who happened to fall in with the
right crowd.

Okay, so technically, my odds of pulling this off may
be no better than that poor little snowball's chance in
hell. But I do have a few tricks up my sleeve, and from
what I've learned, it's all in the presentation. Introduce
my lukewarm twist on their tired old game like it's all
that and then some, and—whammo—mission accom-

plished. They're gonna remember me after tonight. Well, here's hoping anyway . . .

"The rules are that *there are no rules,*" I continue, lowering my voice for dramatic effect. "Nothing is off-limits. Any question—any dare—*everything* is up for grabs."

"I don't know . . ." Alona says, drawing her knees up under her chin. We're all sitting in a circle on her plush pink carpet and, aside from me, everyone's wearing some kind of skimpy, silky, spaghetti-strap nightie thing. You know, like grown women do on TV? I should've known my gray sweats and faded Doors T-shirt wouldn't fly.

"Oh, come on, Lonnie," Grace says, a little glint flickering in her narrow hazel eyes. "You're the one who said you loved danger."

"Well, I do, but . . ." She breaks into a nervous smile. "All right, what the hell. Let's do it."

Now it's Grace's turn to hesitate. "Hold on a second. If there are no rules, how do we play?"

"Good question," I tell her. *And good thing I've already thought of an answer.* "There is a set of directions we'll follow. For each person that takes the hot seat—"

"The hot seat?" Sammie asks cautiously.

"Yeah. Like, say you're first. That means you're in the hot seat, in which case the three of us are free to ask you anything—we *each* get to pick a question. And I don't mean lame-ass shit like 'Who was your first crush?' or 'Do you think so-and-so is cute?' but *real* stuff, stuff we're actually *burning* to know. And you have to answer, no matter how personal it gets."

"But what if she picks Dare?" Grace asks.

"Well, see, the game is more like Truth *and* Dare ... *or* Torture," I tell them.

"Torture?" Alona repeats, her eyes widening. This is good, just the reaction I'd hoped for.

"Don't worry. That part comes later," I say gleefully. "First there's the cross-examination, and when that's over, we all get to put our heads together and come up with something totally crazy for the truth teller to do."

"And no matter what it is, the person has to follow through?" Alona guesses.

"Despite the potentially toxic and humiliating consequences?" Grace adds.

I give them a satisfied smile. "Now you guys are getting the idea. And remember, our only limitations are the boundaries of our warped and sinful minds."

"But what if you won't do it?" Sammie asks. "I mean, what if it's something that, like, goes against your religion?"

"*My* religion?" I say. "Well, luckily I brought my rabbi's phone number with me. I'm sure he'll be glad to let me know what's kosher and what isn't."

"No, seriously, what happens if one of us flat-out refuses?" Alona asks. "Is it 'game over'?"

"Are you kidding?" I say. "The game would just be starting. See, it would be three against one," I explain to them. "Three people who want the person to take the dare, and one who refuses. That's where the torture part comes in."

Grace and Alona exchange glances before setting their mutual sights on me, gawking at me almost as if I'm from another planet . . . but a planet they most definitely like. Sammie, on the other hand, doesn't appear too thrilled.

"Oh, come on, Sammie," I say. "It'll be fun. I used to do this with my friends all the time back home." Lie. I pulled the torture twist out of my ass two nights ago when I should have been studying for my chem exam.

"But when you say *torture,* you mean . . ."

I shrug. "Tickle torture, pinning you down while we burp stale Frappuccino breath in your face, things like that."

"Or we could wait to torture you in front of the entire school," Grace adds with a sinister air. "Mortify you when you're least expecting it."

Sammie looks at me skeptically.

"Don't worry. We're not gonna pour rat poison down your throat if that's what you're thinking," I tell her.

"Cat piss, maybe . . ." Grace says.

We all laugh until Alona, our natural-born ring-leader, clears her throat, silencing us all. "So, Sammie, are you in?"

Sammie nods reluctantly. "Aren't I always?"

Excellent! See? It's just like I told you—all in the presentation. I didn't really just reinvent the oldest party game in sleepover history, but as far as these three are concerned, I'm Thomas Freakin' Edison.

"All right, then," Alona says. "Hey, CG, since it's your game, why don't you go first?"

"No problem," I say eagerly. "Let the interroga-tion begin."

Actually, this is what I wanted—to go first, to have them shine the spotlight on me for a change instead of Alona and her big bag of fabulous. When people have money and looks and popularity and they're actually willing to accept you, don't expect them to turn around and honestly try to get to know you, too. This is my chance for Alona, Sammie, and Grace to finally under-stand what the real CG Silverman is all about. Make that the real CG Silverman minus the boring with a few extra ounces of confetti.

"Okay, I'll start," Sammie says, stretching her baby blue nightgown down over her voluptuous thighs. "Do you think Alona's brother's a hottie?"

"Sammie!" Alona scolds her. "Those are exactly the kinds of lame-ass things CG told us not to ask."

Are you hearing this? Suddenly *I'm* the boss?

"No, it's cool," I say, noticing the shamed expression on Sammie's burnt sienna face. "It's a good warm-up question."

"Well, then?" Grace asks impatiently. "Your answer?"

I smile casually. "I'd do him."

Of course, I'm kidding. I mean, the boy is hotter than the blazing sun in the middle of August, but he's also a nineteen-year-old college sophomore with loads of experience on me, a *high school* sophomore who has never "done it"—or even considered *thinking* about doing it—with anyone. Not even my old best buddy Alex.

"That's disgusting," Alona says. "But since you brought it up, how many guys have you done? Or are you still a virgin?"

"That's two questions in one," I tell her.

"Can I rephrase?" she asks sweetly, batting her curly, long lashes as if the coquettish tactic will have any effect whatsoever on my decision.

"Go ahead." All right, what can I say? The girl has managed to wrap me around her pretty little manicured finger, just like she has everybody else. But it won't be long before she's just as caught up in my world as I am in hers. Starting in five . . . four . . . three . . . two . . .

"So, okay, how far *have* you gotten?" Alona asks.

"Let's just put it this way," I say. "The answer to the second question you asked—before you rephrased—is no." Here it comes . . . "I'm not a virgin."

"Wait a second," Grace blurts incredulously. "You're telling us you've had *sex?* With *who?*"

"Does this count as your question?" I ask.

"Yes, yes!" she exclaims, bopping me on the shoulder with her teddy bear. "My question to you is who in the world did you have sex with and why are we just finding out about it now?"

"Okay, first of all, that's two questions," I say, to which Grace groans, lurching forward as if she's about to strangle me. "But to answer the first one, which I assume is the one you're really dying to know the answer to . . ." I pause to build suspense and notice a wide-eyed trio of stunned faces staring back at me. Geez, is it *that* hard to believe I've done the deed? And does this mean none of *them* have? Not even Alona? "His name was Alex—*is* Alex. We dated all throughout eighth, ninth, and the first half of tenth grade, but I broke things off with him when I moved up here."

Okay, if you want the real truth, Alex and I never went together at all. But the sparks have been flying ever since seventh-grade home ec class when Ms. Cappanelli paired us up for that ridiculous quiche-making contest.

Not exactly the stuff of a steamy romance novel, I know, especially considering the way we spent our time. Alex and I could shoot hoops together, play Xbox, even have burping wars, but when it came to acknowledging the sparks factor, to talking about how we really felt? Forget about it. Would you believe he waited 'til the day before I moved to finally say what we'd both known forever? I told him it was too late, that he'd had three and a half years to ask me out. I said I was ready to experience the world outside the city, to become somebody new, somebody special, and that meant being free to date whoever I wanted, not being tied to some childhood friend from back home. His exact response? "God, I never knew you were such a bitch."

"Why'd you break up with him?" Sammie asks.

"Uh-uh-uh," Alona says. "CG's round of questioning is over."

"No, it's all right," I tell them. I like talking about this new and exciting CG. "If you really want to know, the relationship was just getting too intense for both of us. My mom found one of his love letters and realized we were, you know . . ."

"Sleeping together?" Grace supplies.

I nod, a little thrill rushing through me. I never realized how much fun stretching the truth could be. People respect you more when they realize you've got things to hide. Give yourself layers, secrets—a past juicier than a pregnant orange—and watch even the worthy ones become your faithful followers.

"Your mom must've totally freaked, huh?" Alona asks, raising her symmetrically arched brows in excitement.

I throw my head back, releasing a theatrical sigh. "You don't know the half of it."

"I'll bet I don't," she says, smiling, then turns to Sammie and Grace. "Come on, ladies. Let's go huddle. I think I've got the perfect dare for our little sex kitten, here."

*Gulp.* So maybe there is a downside to this whole pregnant orange business. My heart begins slamming against the walls of my chest like my body's hosting its own sudden-death racquetball match, but there's no turning back now. After all, it's my game.

# four ... or dare

*One more deep breath,* I tell myself, *and then you're doing this.* I can hear the girls giggling down the hall. It's now or never. And there's no way I'm about to chicken out on my own game. Especially when they all think I'm Miss Sex Queen Extraordinaire. Speaking of which, did they *have* to dress me up in Alona's way-too-short, leopard print, babydoll nightie with the matching three-inch stiletto slippers—you know, the kind with the little pompoms on top? They look like something my grandmother would've worn to woo the UPS guy while my granddad was away on business in the '80s. That is, if my grandmother had been a slut.

I knock on his door. *Please be asleep or in some kind of mysterious coma. Be playing with yourself for all I care, just don't answer the freaking—*

"Come in."

Crap!

I twist the knob and carefully tiptoe into the room. And there he is—Sammie and Grace's fantasy man— sitting on his bed in a white undershirt and flannel pajama bottoms, casually reading a book. His wood-paneled walls are decked with posters, from *The Breakfast Club* to the Beatles to some jaw-droppingly suggestive Victoria's Secret spreads. Yeah, I'm sure I can compete with *that*. *Thanks a lot, girls.*

"What's up?" Jordan asks, flashing a curious smile.

I let my eyes linger upon his amazing bone structure, perfectly tousled brown hair, sculpted biceps, and um ... What was the question? "Oh," I stutter, "I, um, just came in to say hi." *Actually, I came in to plunk myself down on your bed, whisper something ridiculously foolish in your ear, and give you a big, fat kiss on the cheek before hauling ass back to your sister's room and announcing that I successfully completed my dare.*

"Oh, well, hi, then," Jordan says, laughing a little as he sets his book down on the nightstand. "Um, nice outfit."

*Oh, this old thing?*

"Thanks," I mumble. "It's Alona's."

"I know. I was with her last summer when she dragged me into Neiman Marcus to buy it." He shakes his head and sighs. "Why any high school girl would willingly dress like a forty-year-old desperate housewife is beyond me."

I laugh. "So I take it you don't always approve of your sister's wardrobe?"

Jordan shrugs. "I think she could take a few lessons from the ladies at Penn State. College girls aren't as preoccupied with their looks. A lot of times, you'll just find them bumming around in sweatpants and T-shirts." He looks at me strangely. "Kind of like what you were wearing earlier tonight when I first met you." A teasing smile slowly spreads across his face. "Oh, God. Don't tell me they stole your soul already."

"So you think I looked better before?" I ask, taking a seat on his bed. Part one of dare: accomplished.

"I don't know about better. Just more natural. And by the way," he says, grinning, "have a seat."

"Oh," I say, trying on one of Alona's coy giggles. "Do you mind?"

Jordan gives me another one of those curious looks and leans forward. At this point, I've gotta be honest—until now, the closest I've ever gotten to such fineness was when I French-kissed my Ashton Kutcher poster four years ago. And Jordan's skin smells a lot sexier than that waxy old roll of paper. "Let me clue you in on a little secret," he says. "No guy in his right mind is going to object to having a half-naked woman climb into his bed at one o'clock in the morning."

Well, I didn't exactly *climb*. And I've never heard anyone refer to me as a *woman* before, but with that said, is Jordan Spelton—King of All Hotties—trying to tell me something here? Is he—dare I say it—*flirting* with me?

"So, why'd you really come in here?" he asks. And may I note that he hasn't backed away yet.

"I, um . . ." *I think you're really sexy. That's all you have to say. Just lean a little closer and whisper in his ear, "I think you're really sexy," and voilà—part two of dare: accomplished.* "I think . . ."

I think Jordan has his hand on my knee.

"What are you doing?" I ask.

"Same thing you are," he whispers, kissing my cheek. "Getting to know an attractive stranger."

"But, wait," I say breathlessly, gently moving his hand away. "I was supposed to kiss *you* on the cheek."

Jordan lets out a quiet little laugh. "Sorry?"

"I was supposed to come in here in this sexy outfit and tell you how sexy I think *you* are and give you this big, fat, wet kiss on the cheek and then . . ." As the oxygen slowly returns to my brain, I realize what a babbling idiot I've become. But Jordan's smoldering blue eyes are full of understanding. How can he not think I'm crazy?

"So, you came in here to seduce me?" he asks, smiling

suggestively. "Only now you're upset because I started seducing you first?" He reaches out to tuck a loose strand of hair behind my ear, and my whole body turns to Jell-O.

"Uh, yeah, sure," I say, forgetting all about the dare, no longer in control of my own impulses. "That's what happened."

"Well, I hope you're not too mad at me," Jordan whispers, cupping my face in his hands. He smells like aftershave, bar soap, and . . . what's that other smell? Oh yeah . . . *man.* All the other guys I've hooked up with—all four of them—have been boys, but Jordan is definitely a man. He's over eighteen. He's in freaking college, for God's sake! He's old enough to vote, fight in the army, rent porno . . . and I can't even drive yet. Holy shit, what am I doing here?

Having the most passionate, intense, wildly heart-stopping, *they could make a love song out of this* kiss I've ever had in my life. That's what. I used to secretly fantasize about doing this kind of thing with Alex. Not that he'd have known how to make a move on me, even if all humankind depended on it. I mean, seriously, the closest we ever got to physical was when he slapped me on the ass during a game of one-on-one. You know, that "way to go, bro" smack that comes with a built-in nonsexual disclaimer and is about as romantic as watching a cow take a crap. Jordan, on the flip side, knows what he's do-ing. And he's pretty damn freaking good at it.

He touches my knee again, and soon those nineteen-year-old hands are traveling toward places I know they shouldn't. I grab hold of his wrists, sliding them away from the danger zone. Taking the hint well, Jordan be-gins to play with my hair, then pulls away from our lip-lock and starts kissing my neck . . .

"God, you're so hot," he whispers. "What's your name again?"

# five keeping secrets

I didn't tell the gang about my little makeout session with Jordan. Okay, make that my *major* makeout session with Jordan. Instead, I was able to explain away all our alone time by saying we spent my postdare wrap-up dissecting his Victoria's Secret fetish. "I know conversation wasn't part of the dare," I told them, "but his obsession really piqued my curiosity. I mean, what's up with those hos, anyway?"

I only lied because I knew Alona would feel weird about it. I mean, I wouldn't want to hear about one of my friends making out with *my* older brother. Not that I have an older brother. Or a younger brother. Or any siblings at all. But that's beside the point. The point (and I do have one) is that I literally cannot stop thinking about him. Not even when I try to force myself. You know that feeling you get when you clench your butt cheeks together to avoid an explosive public fart? But the gas still bubbles up inside you and makes an embarrassing gurgling sound anyway? Well, I guess my feelings for Jordan have become like that public fart—overwhelming, noisy, and almost impossible to control. They rumble from my tummy down to my toes every time I remember his kiss. Which is essentially every waking, dreaming, and breathing moment.

I've been dying to tell someone—*anyone*—about my freaking fantabulous experience with the most beautiful boy—ahem, make that *man*—this suburb has ever seen. But as you can understand, my options have been limited. Until now. I mean, who better to tell than a girl who has no chance in hell of ever spilling my secret, a girl more likely to be abducted by aliens than accepted by Alona Spelton's posse? A girl like . . .

"Glory!" I call to the lanky beanpole in the oversized parka who has just stepped off the school bus. "Glory Finklefuss, right?" I've made a habit out of walking three or four paces behind her so we'd never accidentally be forced to converse on our way home. But today is different. Today I'm in a talkative kind of mood.

She turns around slowly, gawking at me with a blank—and almost terrified—stare. Um, can anybody say *deer in headlights*?

"Yeah," she finally manages to say. "I'm Glory Finkle-fuss. How'd you know?"

I shrug. "We *are* neighbors. I've been meaning to introduce myself for a while now. It's just that you always speed off that bus so fast, I never get a chance to say hi."

"Oh." Long . . . excruciating . . . pause. "Well, I know who *you* are." Is that contempt I'm hearing in her voice? "You're friends with Alona Spelton and all them, aren't you?"

"Yeah, but . . ." *I know exactly what it's like to be you. To be . . . invisible.*

"But I guess you're different from them," she says, her beady brown eyes giving me the once-over.

"Why do you say that?" I ask.

"You're talking to me, aren't you?"

I can't help but smile. "So, you're saying my friends are snobs?"

"Not snobs," Glory says, the early February wind whipping through her frizzy orange mane. "Just exclusive."

"No arguments there," I confess, following her lead as she turns to resume her homeward journey.

"So, how come you don't look like them?" Glory asks. "I mean, I used to be friends with Samara and Grace in middle school and—"

"You *were*?" I blurt. *Okay, note to self: Next time the class nerd tells you she wasn't* always *the class nerd, don't go into labor in the middle of the street.* "I mean, they never mentioned it."

"Well of course they haven't. People go their separate ways in high school. That's what happens." She looks down at her feet, and I recognize that her shoes are from Payless, just like mine. "So, how come you don't look like them?" she repeats, glancing back up at me.

"You mean, how come I don't dress like Paris Hilton?"

Glory laughs. It's a familiar laugh, even though I've never heard it before. It kind of makes me miss Alex— the way he'd fall down chuckling at just about anything I said even if it wasn't that funny. The Four Tops—we have fun, but not in that easy, lighthearted way that just makes you want to crack up at the world. Sometimes I wish Alex would just pick up the goddamn phone and call me already. Not that I know what I'd say to him.

"Well, Samara and Grace didn't dress like Paris, either," Glory says. "Not until we all got to high school and they met Alona—you know she went to a different middle school than us—and once that happened, I just sort of got kicked to the curb."

"Well, sorry about that. To be honest, though, guys don't really go for the whole Paris Hilton thing, anyway. They like a girl who can just kick it in a pair of baggy pants," I say, subtly indicating my oversized corduroys, "and an old, beat-up T-shirt."

Glory gives me a funny look. "So, is that why you're the rebel of the group? 'Cause you're all about trying to impress the boys?"

Me, a *rebel*? CG Silverman—all-American, freckle-faced Jewish girl; Miss Ordinary; chubby-cheeked, doe-eyed, fish-out-of-water scaredy-cat; world's biggest wannabe. *A rebel?*

"I couldn't care less about *boys,*" I tell her, shrugging carelessly as I bend down to retrieve an empty Pepsi can from the sidewalk. "There's this college man I'm seeing, and he thinks it's totally sexy when I go casual." I swing my arm back as if I'm about to make the perfect pitch, then end up chucking the can at a nearby garden statue. "Don't you just hate lawn decorations?" I say, playing up my new rebel image.

"Uh, I guess so."

"They completely piss me off."

"So, wait," Glory says as we round the corner of our street. "Who's this college guy you're seeing?"

"Just some dude up at Penn State. Actually, if you swear not to say anything, I'll tell you his name."

She gives me a strange look. "Is it someone I know?"

"Not exactly, but once I tell you his name, you'll realize why it's such a big secret."

Glory smiles. "I should inform you, I'm *really* good at keeping secrets."

"Well, this one's major," I say. "And I'm dying to tell somebody. But it's freaking cold as Alaska out here. You wanna come over and help me raid my parents' fridge or something? And I can tell you all about my boyfriend?"

She looks at me skeptically as we turn onto the narrow walkway that leads to my little gray townhouse. "You mean members of the Four Tops actually pig out?"

"Hey, I'm the rebel of the group, remember?"

"How could I forget? You're dating a college guy and you just invited one of the biggest geeks at Beaubridge to come hang out with you after school. You obviously don't care what anyone thinks."

I step up onto our tiny concrete porch, sighing deeply. *If only that were true . . .*

# SIX boyfriend schmoyfriend

So, I know what you're thinking: I lied to Glory Finkle-fuss. But, in one sense, I told her the truth—she knows who my mystery college man is now and why it's so important we keep our relationship under wraps. I just failed to mention that one itty bitty, *oh-so-trivial* techni-cality: the fact that Jordan and I don't actually *have* a re-lationship. But, trust me, that won't be the case for long. And besides, the truth is always more fun when you stretch it. Glory looked like she'd swallowed a bomb af-ter I revealed the name of my secret paramour. Does it get any more fun than *that?*

"Was that *Glory Finklefuss* I saw you talking to before homeroom this morning?" Alona asks as we all sit scarf-ing down our midday meals at our VIP table in the center of the cafeteria.

"Well, it wasn't Osama bin Laden," I tease. "Although

you say her name as if it was." Okay, so that last part I muttered under my breath, but not quite quietly enough for it to go unheard.

"Oh, we're sorry," Grace snaps. "We didn't realize it was Adopt-a-Freak week."

"Grace . . ." Alona cautions.

You'd think that with all her magnetism and clout, not to mention her hundreds of admirers, Alona would be the bitchy one. But from what I've seen in the last five weeks, she really isn't bitchy at all, just overindulged. And exclusive, like Glory said. I guess she feels the same way about geeks and ugly people as today's hillbilly conservatives feel about "them homosexuals"—they have every right in the world to exist as long as they don't actually expect equal treatment. Grace, on the other hand, can turn on the "bitch switch" like no one I've ever seen. Then again, she also has a much bigger, brighter, sassier, sexier, and wittier personality than our fair leader. Which makes me wonder why she's never tried to overthrow her. And then, of course, there's Sammie. I glance over at my tangerine-tinted pal, wondering what her reaction is to all this. Naturally, she has none.

Alona turns to me. "We just didn't realize you were friends with her, that's all."

"Well, we're not *friends*." Come on, would *you* admit it? "But we do live on the same street," I say, shrugging.

"We're bound to talk now and then." I want to bring up what Glory told me—about her Three Musketeers days with Sammie and Grace—but I'm still pretty new to this clique. Ruffle the wrong feathers too soon and I could find myself sitting at Glory's lunch table tomorrow afternoon with the rest of the "freaks and geeks." Not that I haven't been enjoying our secret little bond, but being in with the right crowd—being *somebody* and standing out—is all I've ever dreamed of. Besides, losing my place in the Four Tops would destroy my chances of ever getting together with Jordan again.

"Oh, hey, CG," Alona says brightly after chugging back a sip of her Evian. "I was talking to my brother after school yesterday and he asked about you."

Okaaaay . . . heart attack! *Just play it cool, you idiot. None of them know what happened, unless of course . . .*

"He told me—"

"He *told* you?"

Alona gives me a puzzled look. "He told me," she resumes from the beginning, "that he thought you were really funny the other night."

Oh. Well, whoopidy-fartin'-doo. No, really, stop the presses. I think the editors at *Cosmo Girl* might even be interested in this one, in documenting how the hottest guy in the world, a guy who could have said anything about me after the other night—from what luscious lips

I have to how mesmerizingly beautiful my eyes are—chose *funny.*

"Well, I'd think it was pretty funny, too, if some strange girl *I'd* just met plunked herself down on *my* bed, whispered sweet nothings in *my* ear, and kissed *me* on the cheek," Grace says, munching on a carrot stick.

"I betcha his girlfriend wouldn't have found it so funny," Sammie says dryly.

*Girlfriend?*

"Uh, I didn't know your brother was seeing anyone," I tell Alona, hoping they'll all mistake the waver in my voice for some sudden sensitivity to chunky peanut butter.

"Oh, come on," Grace says. "You've never heard the expression 'All the good ones are taken'?"

"No, I have." I was just too naïve and immature to understand what it actually meant. Now I know.

# seven the love doctor is in

I haven't told anyone about my broken heart. Alona, Sammie, and Grace keep wanting to know why I've been so down in the dumps, but I just tell them it's PMS (short, of course, for Pity Myself Syndrome). It's times like this that I really miss Alex. He always knew just what to say to make me feel better. Even if it was just making fun of whoever was on my shit list, long enough for me to realize they weren't worth getting upset over in the first place. But I could never imagine coming to that conclusion about Jordan. He's just too . . . *hot*. And godly. And perfect. Besides, he's the first guy I've ever really, seriously, passionately made out with. How could I not have feelings for him? How could I not be crushed? Still, I wonder what Alex would say if I told him. If we were still best friends . . . Meanwhile, Glory keeps asking about my sizzling adult relationship with a certain college man upstate. I can't exactly let her down, so I've been embellishing a bit, just on the absolute essentials— you know, like our "four-hour phone conversation" the other night and the way his voice caresses my name whenever he says the words "I love you, Cynthia Gene." Little things like that.

I've always heard that the best way to get over some- one is to set your sights on someone new, but what can I say? Jordan Spelton has spoiled me for other guys. If I can't have him, I'd just as soon become a nun. A fifteen- year-old Jewish nun.

"So, ladies, I think it's about time I told you why we're here." That would be Alona speaking, and *here* would be Café Starlight, an upscale little coffee shop that makes Starbucks look like the Walmart cafeteria. Alona decided this would be the perfect place for the Four Tops to spend our Saturday afternoon, huddled around her fluorescent pink laptop while sipping funky- colored tea that tastes like feet.

"Well, *I*, for one, am dying to know," Grace says, giv- ing me a little wink. Despite her general air of bitchi- ness, we seem to have an unspoken understanding. It's as if, in a world where the vast majority of our peers be- lieve those MTV reality shows are totally unscripted and the Simpson sisters really *do* have talent, we're the only two people who actually get the joke.

"Well . . ." Alona begins, turning her gaze toward me. "We all know our little CG has had a terrible case of the miseries lately. And *I* thought, what better way to pull her up out of those nasty premenstrual blues than with a little game of chatty-chat on the Net." She smiles brightly, glancing from Grace to Sammie and then back to me again. "What do you think?"

"Wait a second," Sammie says. "Is this like the time we . . ."

Alona nods slowly. Mischievously. "Exactly."

Grinning, Grace reaches out to pat my hand. "Well, she is our little daredevil. I mean, she did go into Jordan's room wearing less than—"

Oh, not this again. "Okay, okay, what am I doing exactly?" I ask impatiently.

Alona motions for me to lean in closer, and with a few simple clicks of her mouse, everything is made clear.

"Single and Looking?" I ask, reading the name of the chat room that has popped up on her laptop screen. The girls giggle.

"Most of them are old, or they'd be in one of the teen rooms," Grace says. "Although there are plenty of pervs on those boards, too."

"Here," Alona says, placing her fingers on the keyboard, "we've gotta register you with a screen name. How about . . ." She thinks for a second.

"Double D," Grace chimes in, "but spell it D-e-e, like the name. It's cuter."

"Clever," Alona applauds, playfully bumping Grace's shoulder. She races through the sign-on process, then slides the laptop over to me. "All right, you sexy *biatch*. Make one of these horny losers fall in love with you."

Wait just a second here. I thought this whole dare or die thing was supposed to be *my* game. How come Alona suddenly gets to take control? Because she's *Alona,* that's why. When she says jump, I'm supposed to say, "Off what bridge?" And as the designated daredevil of the group, it's not within my contract rights to chicken out or ask questions. So here goes nothing . . .

"Well, this guy looks promising," I joke, pointing the cursor at some poor schmo who had the unfortunate stroke of "genius" to choose the screen name Loves_ Me_The_Booty.

"How do you know that's a guy?" Grace asks suggestively.

"Um, ew," Sammie groans.

"Well, it *is* a coed chat room," Grace reminds her. Then, facing me, she adds, "And I think you should go for her . . . him . . . *it*." She turns to Alona. "Right, Lon? I mean, your only requirement was that CG snag a horny loser. You never specified which gender."

Alona shrugs. "Yeah, I guess you're right." She pats my shoulder. "Go for it, you big stud. Send that booty lover a private message."

"Ooh, hold on a second," Grace says, stopping me. "What do we have here?"

What we have is a private message of our own—sent to DoubleDee by a certain Doctor_Love. These people really have to come up with better screen names. And while they're at it, better lives.

```
Doctor_Love: asl?
```

"Oh, do you believe this?" I say. "We haven't even exchanged two words and he's already asking for ass? Nice *typo,* by the way. No wonder this guy has to seek companionship over the Internet."

Alona laughs. "Asl means 'age/sex/location.' God, CG, haven't you ever been in a chat room before?"

"Not *this* kind of chat room," I admit. Although to be honest, with only one computer in the house, I don't exactly have much time for surfing naughty websites. Let's face it, in this creepy world of stalker Net loons who prey upon innocent teens like me, I'm every parent's wildest dream—who's about to be corrupted right before your very eyes.

"Tell him—or *her*," Grace says, reminding me that this feel-good practitioner might turn out to be about as masculine as Dr. Ruth, "that you're twenty-five and from somewhere totally urban like New York or LA."

I take a deep breath, followed by a swig of my foot-flavored tea, and start typing.

```
DoubleDee: I'm 25, from NYC, and as for
sex . . . Do you know any self-respecting
MAN who would call himself "DoubleDee"?
Unless, of course, you don't get the play
on words.
Doctor_Love: LOL. No, I get it. I love
puns. Some people think it's dorky, but
I'm a high school Honors English teacher.
Words are my life. Puns, metaphors, saucy
innuendoes—it's all foreplay to me.
```

*"Saucy?"* Grace exclaims. "Who *talks* like that? Ew, ask him—well, first make sure it *is* a him—then, ask if all Honors English teachers are really closet sex freaks."

"Yeah, you wish," I say with a giggle. Grace and I are both enrolled in the Honors English program at Beau-bridge, and our teacher, Mr. Fenowitz, is a major fox.

As far as teachers go, anyway. Grace isn't in my class, though, so we've never actually had the privilege of drooling over him together.

```
DoubleDee: Asl?
Doctor_Love: 29, male, town not worth
mentioning
```

"Ask him my question," Grace urges. "I'm serious. I wanna know if Mr. F will get off on my 'saucy' take on *The Iliad* when I turn in my paper next week."

"I'm not gonna ask him if all Honors English teachers are undercover word pervs."

"Yeah, come on," Alona says. "Let CG handle it. It's her dare. And after all, she *is* our resident seductress."

Folding her arms across her chest, Grace resigns herself to a spectator's role and sighs. I keep on typing.

```
DoubleDee: So this town of yours . . . How
come it's not worth mentioning?
Doctor_Love: Well, compared with New York
City, is any town worth mentioning?
DoubleDee: LOL. So tell me what state
you're from, then.
Doctor_Love: PA. And if you really want
```

> to know the name of my town—although I'm
> willing to bet dollars to doughnuts you've
> never heard of it—I'll tell you that, too.
> **DoubleDee:** Shoot. I just might prove
> you wrong.
> **Doctor_Love:** Okay, then . . . It's a small
> suburb about 45 minutes north of Philly
> called Beaubridge. Ring any bells?

Holy tea funk! I turn to face the girls, whose jaws have all just dropped into their fancy Café Starlight mugs, same as mine.

"Doctor Love . . . is from around *here?*" Sammie articulates slowly.

Grace shakes her head in giddy disbelief. "Doctor Love is *Mr. Fenowitz.*"

"Oh, come on," I say, fighting for a lost cause. "He said he was from Beaubridge. He never said he taught at Beaubridge *High.*"

"And how many high schools are there in Beaubridge?" Grace asks, raising her eyebrows.

"One," I say meekly. And this, my friends, is why it's a lost cause. I mean, I don't care how cute the man is. He's still my teacher. And I know things about him now I wish I didn't. Like the fact that he spends his free time lurking in chat rooms waiting for playful puns and "saucy innuendoes" to saunter by and stroke his fiddle.

"Well, maybe it's a different teacher," Alona says brightly, sensing my ickiness. "I know a couple juniors in the Honors English program and they don't have this Fenowitz guy."

"True," Grace says. "They have Berman. *Mrs.* Berman. Sixty-something, grandmother of seven, church club president Mrs. Berman. I hardly think she's 'single and looking' for twenty-five-year-old city girls with double D breasts."

"You never know," I say.

An instant message suddenly appears at the bottom of the screen.

**JAS88:** What's up, loser?

"Who's that?" I ask.

Alona rolls her eyes. "Oh, it's just my brother. Ignore him."

*Yeah, as if* that's *humanly possible.*

Doctor_Love: Are you still there?

"Oh, God," I say, cringing.

"Face it, Ceej," Grace tells me. "Out of all the horny

losers in cyberspace, you managed to seduce our *teacher.*"
She smiles, giving me one of her signature winks. "You
really are a pro, aren't you?"

**JAS88:** Earth to my bimbonic sister!

*JAS88, huh? Good to know . . .*
"A pro?" I repeat nonchalantly. "Hardly. I'm just
learning as I go."

# *eight* how i learned to juggle

By definition, juggling is keeping two or more objects in the air at once by alternately tossing and catching them. This sometimes involves a little trickery—*particularly* when those objects are men.

I started to become fluent in this complex, ancient art the night I hijacked the family computer to set the record straight with Jordan. Or more precisely, to find out why in the world that good-for-nothing but oh-so-devastatingly-fine piece of horse manure would kiss me—make that *sweep me off my rebellious little feet*—if he already had a girlfriend. I didn't expect things to go smoothly, but I definitely wasn't thinking they'd turn out like *this*.

It happened exactly thirty-six hours ago, just after I got back from Alona's house. Sammie, Grace, and I were invited to have dinner there following my secret "love chat" with Mr. Saucy Innuendo at the café (an event I was more than positive I'd never live down). I told my parents I was planning to meet the girls online for a little gabfest—believe me, they'd never have bought the "research paper" excuse on a Saturday night—and disappeared into my father's office to begin stalking my college cutie. Who most likely had better things to do than spend *his* Saturday night holed up behind a computer monitor. Or maybe not ...

### JAS88 has signed on

I don't know the exact number of beats my heart skipped, but I do know that if I hadn't been so dead set on ambushing the sexiest man alive, I definitely would have taken the time to call 911.

**JJ_Pearl:** Hey, stranger ...
**JAS88:** Who is this?

To be honest, I wasn't expecting him to have a clue. At least not from my screen ID, which happens to be a tribute to the greatest recording artist of all time, Janis Joplin (*JJ* obviously representing her initials, and *Pearl* stemming from her posthumously released album, which was titled after her self-given nickname . . . in case you were wondering). I totally ripped the idea off of Alex, whose screen name, JH_r-u-experienced, is a shout-out to the *second*-greatest recording artist of all time, Jimi Hendrix. Although the Jimi vs. Janis debate was ongoing, our mutual love for classic rock—and combined revulsion toward the bubble-gum pop that's soiled the ears of our generation—was just one of the many things Alex and I had in common. Before we went our separate ways. Christ, he'd be cringing like an old man's ass during a prostate exam if he ever heard the sugary, synthesized crap Alona, Grace, and Sammie listen to. But enough about my former BFF (emphasis on the *former*). It was time to focus on the future and let Jordan in on my true identity—or at least give him another chance to try to figure it out.

> **JJ_Pearl:** Guess.
> **JAS88:** Do I get a hint?
> **JJ_Pearl:** Um, let's just say we got to know each other pretty well in your room one night not too long ago.
> **JAS88:** Uh . . . can I get a better hint than that?

*What?* How many girls did he make out with that weekend? *Oh, wait, he's probably thinking* dorm *room,* I told myself. But still, wasn't this guy supposed to have a *girlfriend?*

> **JJ_Pearl:** You're a total player, aren't you?
>
> **JAS88:** Aren't *you?* You took your chances. You knew my situation.
>
> **JJ_Pearl:** "Situation" meaning you were taken?
>
> **JAS88:** Come on, baby. Don't get all sanctimonious on me now. We both had a good time. I didn't hear you complaining that night.
>
> **JJ_Pearl:** You don't even know who I am!
>
> **JAS88:** Sure, I do. You're every girl. You're all the same. No complaints during, nothing but "wa wa wa" after. I never told you I'd be your boyfriend.
>
> **JJ_Pearl:** I never asked you to be! But it would've been nice to know you were *somebody's* boyfriend before we did what we did.
>
> **JAS88:** Don't play dumb. Everyone knows I have a girlfriend at Stanford. Ask any girl at this school and she'll tell you I'm with Cassandra.

Cassandra, hmm? It's always nice to know the name of thine enemy. Although I guess she could say the same thing about me.

**JJ_Pearl:** And what makes you think I go to "this school"?

**JAS88:** ?

**JJ_Pearl:** Haven't you ever cheated on Cassandra during a visit *home* from Penn State?

No answer.

**JJ_Pearl:** Like, say, with one of your sister's friends?

**JAS88:** LOL! Grace, don't ever do that to me again.

*Grace?* Since when did Jordan and *Grace* start fooling around? And why didn't she ever say anything about it? Perhaps for the same reason I didn't . . .

**JAS88:** Why'd you change your screen name?

*What screen name are you referring to, jackass?* I can hardly see it through all these fat, soggy tears of mine.

**JJ_Pearl:** I'm not Grace.

No answer again.

**JJ_Pearl:** I guess you don't remember a freckle-faced brunette in a leopard-print nightie coming in at one in the morning to sit on your bed?

### JAS88 has signed off at 9:37 p.m.

Damn it! I thought I was supposed to be the one with all the street smarts—the kind of kid who could smell trouble brewing from a mile away—but I guess no amount of city living can prepare you for high school in the big, bad 'burbs. Where being fake is a survival skill. And keeping secrets is a way of life.

I was in the middle of bawling my eyes out when my mother tapped on the door. Perfect. What in the world was I supposed to tell *her?*

"Oh, honey, what's the matter?" she wanted to know as soon as she entered the room and saw what a wreck I was. I had to think fast.

"Alona's turtle died!" *Good one, huh?* "It was all so sudden!" I buried my head against her poochy, premeno-pausal belly and continued to sob. "You should've known him, Mom. He was, like, the coolest turtle *ever!*"

"Aw," my mother said gently. "You must be thinking of Maxie, huh?"

*Maxie, that's right!* My childhood cat that died four years ago. I'd heard about this. It's called method acting—relies heavily on emotional recall. Alona's heart-wrenching "turtle tragedy" (wink, wink) had gone and triggered a painful pet memory of my very own. How totally *genius!*

"Yes, Maxie!" I wailed. "I miss her so much!"

My mother pulled away from me, crinkling her brow. "Maxie was a *boy.*" *Oops.* "But try not to think about that old guy," she said, wiping my tears away, "because Alona's on the phone now, and she sounds just fine."

"She's on the phone *now?*" I asked, struggling to pull myself together.

"Mmm-hmm." My mom smiled. "I don't see why you gals make such a big deal about chatting online if you're just gonna end up calling each other to talk live anyway."

"Um . . ." *Crap.* My girly gabfest excuse for hijacking the family PC.

"Well, I guess she's just upset about her turtle and wanted to hear a friendly voice," my mother reasoned.

"Yeah," I said thankfully as she turned to leave the room. *Good save, Mom.* "That must be it."

Now, how in the world was I supposed to talk to Alona without mentioning the meager weensy fact that her slimy (yet ironically delicious) brother had just performed a lethal hit and run on my heart? And what about Grace? Should I tell her about Grace? Because if you want to know the truth, I was fuming at the thought of that oversexed little hussy slobbering all over my man. *My* man. Hah! He's *everybody's* man. Until he blows them off to play the role of Mr. Committed.

"Hey, Lon," I said, picking up the phone. "What's up?"

"Hey," she began, "I wanted to ask you—"

"Wait, hold on," I interrupted, hearing my mom on the extension. "Mom, I've got it. You can hang up."

"Okay," my mother said. "But first, Alona, I just want to tell you how sorry I am for your loss."

"My loss?"

"I heard he was a wonderful turtle."

And with that beautiful sentiment, my mother put down the phone.

Alona giggled nervously. "*What* was she talking about?"

"Don't ask."

"Too late."

*Come on, rebel girl,* I told myself, *you can do it. You've become quite the expert at telling lies.*

"Uh . . . I got a really emotional e-mail from Alex tonight," I fumbled. "You know, my ex?"

"You mean, the one you were sleeping with?"

See what I mean? Our world leaders should be taking lessons in duplicity from me.

"Yeah. It was really disturbing," I told her. "He ended

up writing some stuff that made me cry and then my mom walked in, and—"

"And you didn't want her to know you were crying over the guy she practically forced you to break up with in the first place."

"Exactly."

"So you made up some lameoid excuse about my turtle kicking the bucket? Even though I've never even had a turtle?" She giggled. "It's okay. I'm sure I would've done something like that, too."

Whew. Crisis averted. Well, at least that one particular crisis. I'd lost count of how many I was going through.

"So, are you planning to get back together with him?" Alona asked.

"Oh, God no," I said. "Nothing like that. He's way too into me. If you want the truth, he's starting to sound a little unstable."

For shit's sake, could I have painted Alex to be any more of a soggy, whiny psychodork? He'd never in a million years be *that* guy. He'd be the guy on the other end of the phone listening to me make fun of *that* guy. That is, if we still spoke to each other. Which we don't. So, what does it matter *how* I paint him?

"Then, why the tears?" Alona asked. "Oh, wait, never mind. I know."

"You *do?*" *Gulp.*

"I swear, CG, you need to get that PMS of yours under control. It's the worst case I've ever seen! Totally over the top."

"That's right!" I said thankfully. My hormonal justification for moping around over her filthy, lying bastard of a brother. Periods and reptiles make such dandy little coverups, don't they? "I'll have to work on that."

"Of course, I'm only telling you this as a friend, not to sound like some kind of know-it-all monster. And with that in mind, I hope you won't think I'm a terrible person for bringing this up either, but ... did you notice how much Sammie had to *eat* tonight?"

Oh, geez. I hadn't realized this was a matter of national urgency.

"Sammie? No, not really," I admitted. "Why? What's the matter?"

"Well, it's just that ..." She trailed off momentarily, sighing into the receiver. "Don't you think she's a little ..."

"Tan?" I offered.

"Big."

*Oh, believe me,* I wanted to say, *that's the least of her problems.* But that would've been cruel, and besides, who *isn't* big compared with Alona? If I didn't know better, I'd swear she was the lost Olsen triplet.

"She's not *big*-big," I said. "She's just bigger boned than you are."

"She's bigger boned than half the school."

"Well, she's tall, too. And voluptuous."

"You mean 'chunky,'" Alona insisted.

"No, not *chunky*. Just . . . full." Exactly, um, *why* were we having this conversation?

"You're being too kind, but that's sort of why I'm coming to you."

"You want me to tell Sammie she's a heifer?" I asked, completely dumbfounded. Which, I've gotta say, was a sweet relief from being completely devastated.

"Well, not in so many words," Alona said. "But yes . . . sort of."

I couldn't help but laugh. "That's one of the oddest requests I've ever heard! And I'm sorry, but as much as I want to help you, Lonnie, I just can't do it."

"Oh, but come on, you can do anything. You're the ballsiest chick I know."

*Ah, here we go again with the courage crap.*

"Look, if you want a rebel, I'm your girl," I told her. "But why intentionally hurt someone's feelings?"

"Hey, I'm not Grace," Alona said. "I don't say things just to be mean."

What was this? A little intraclique cattiness going on

right before my very ears? You mean to tell me our queen bee actually knows her most fashionable accessory—that being her most glamorous sidekick—isn't perfect? Moreover, that she's a downright brother-humping, boyfriend-stealing bitch from hell? Oh, wait a second. *I* added that last part. Never mind.

"In fact," Alona continued, "that's why I'm not going to Grace about this. I mean, she's gutsy, too—"

"But not like me," I interjected. Hey, Grace already had Jordan. I wasn't about to let the little snotrag steal my daredevil reputation, too. "You know as well as anybody that I've never backed down from a dare."

"Well, I know, but this isn't a *dare,* really. It's just that I need one of Sammie's friends—someone with spunk who knows how to tell it like it is without being hurtful—to make her understand that we notice." The thing about Alona is that she really *does* mean well. Her causes just happen to be totally mindless, trivial, and insignificant. That's all.

"Notice what? That she wasn't blessed with a fast metabolism and perfect genes? I'm sure she already knows that," I said, my head suddenly filled with images of Sammie sucking in her belly and yanking at her clothes in an effort to conceal those areas of her body she'd rather keep hidden from the world.

"Yeah, but it's something she could work on," Alona pressed. "I mean, she ate *four* slices of pizza tonight. You only had two, and Grace and I had just one apiece."

"Okay . . . But you also have to remember she's feeding a much bigger person."

"My point exactly."

"I didn't mean it that way. What I'm saying is, how tall is she? Five foot ten? She's got, like, seven or eight inches on the rest of us." Believe me, I'm really not as dumb as this conversation makes me sound.

"CG, my *dad* never even has four slices. And did you see the way she ran to the bathroom afterward? It's like she porked out so bad, she induced diarrhea." Gorgeous image there.

"Okay, I'll talk to her," I resolved finally. "Providing you never mention that diarrhea thing again."

"Deal." I could literally hear the smile in her voice. Alona really is a sweet person. I'm just waiting for the day when she turns three-dimensional. "Well, I'll let you get back to your e-mail from Alex," she said. "Try not to let it get to you, though, all right? Remember, all guys seem like the One when you're PMS-ing. At least that's how I get. Totally sappy and sentimental, not to mention horny."

We both giggled.

"Believe me," I said, "I know Alex isn't the One." *But if you really want to adopt a worthy cause, you could talk to that scumbucket brother of yours for me.*

"Well, remember what they say: Knowing is half the battle. Peace out, Ceej."

"Talk to you later."

After hanging up with Alona, I found myself staring at a dormant computer screen, all cried out for the moment but feeling worse than when I first found out about Jordan and Grace, even more dejected than when, upon discovering my true identity, he split like the crotch on a fat man's pants. I'd sort of been hoping that during Alona's and my lengthy—and meaningless—phone conversation, JAS88 would've signed back on. If only so that I could give him a piece of my mind. (And then provide him with the opportunity to change it.) But no such luck.

So, tell me, if you were depressed and lonely and looking for a little something to numb the pain while you *didn't* wait for a certain someone to *maybe* reappear online, if in the heartbroken haze of a Saturday night, with Monday seeming so far away, you were feeling just the slightest bit adventurous and happened to remember a teensy harmless flirtation with a certain adorable teacher who might actually be wasting away in cyberspace, too—a victim of his own loneliness—would you go for it? I thought so.

Of course, I only intended to look. To see if Doctor_
Love was online. But after logging on to that Single and
Looking chat room using the silly DoubleDee screen
name Streetwalker Grace had come up with, and realizing that there was, in fact, a doctor in the house, I just
couldn't resist seeing if he remembered me. I guess, after
realizing how insignificant I'd been to Jordan, I just
wanted to feel important to *someone*. So, without overthinking it, I instantly began typing.

> DoubleDee: Hey there.
> Doctor_Love: What's happening, city girl?
> No special plans tonight?

*Nope, I'm just as big a loser as you are.*

> DoubleDee: I'm meeting up with some
> friends later.
> Doctor_Love: I see . . . Going clubbing?

*Is that what single, big-busted, twenty-five-year-old New
Yorkers do?*

> DoubleDee: Yup
> Doctor_Love: Well, just remember to save
> the last dance for me.

Suddenly, I had a vision of Mr. Fenowitz as my home-coming date—his soft, curly mop of sandy blond hair framing his gentle boyish face as he stood in my parents' foyer, nervously clutching the corsage he'd bought for me. His tall, lanky body barely filling out his tux . . . There was something soothing about the image, something that made me want to just reach through that dusty old computer monitor and hug the hell out of him.

DoubleDee: Maybe one of these days we could go dancing together.

*Did I really just say that?*

DoubleDee: You seem like a really nice guy.
Doctor_Love: I am a really nice guy. I've just always had trouble meeting really nice girls.
DoubleDee: Ahem.
Doctor_Love: Present company excluded.
DoubleDee: Thank you.
Doctor_Love: So, isn't this a shame?
DoubleDee: A shame?
Doctor_Love: Well, here we have a really nice guy and a really nice girl, and they don't even know each other's names.

*Crap. Nothing like putting me on the spot. Um . . . CG, CG, Bo, BeeGee, Banana Fana, Fo . . .*

    DoubleDee: Fiji
    Doctor_Love: Uh, sorry?
    DoubleDee: Fiji. That's my name.

*Great job, retardo. How you gonna explain that one?*

    Doctor_Love: Like the islands?
    DoubleDee: Exactly!

*And thank you, Doctor_Love.*

    DoubleDee: Rumor has it that's where I
    was conceived. Of course, my parents had
    no way of predicting I'd turn out to be
    as hot and exotic as the islands I was
    named after.
    Doctor_Love: LOL!

*Hot damn! I'm actually surprisingly good at this, I realized. Who knew?*

    DoubleDee: And your name is?
    Doctor_Love: Really boring.

DoubleDee: Well, it's nice to meet you, Really Boring.

Doctor_Love: Ha ha. I meant my name is really boring compared with yours. It's Bill.

DoubleDee: Well, that's just really boring. Period.

Doctor_Love: I was named after my father, William Arthur, who died in a car crash three months before I was born.

*Okay, open mouth. Insert Chewbacca's left foot.*

Doctor_Love: Gotcha.☺

DoubleDee: So, wait, that *didn't* happen?

Doctor_Love: Nah. At least not to me. I just figured we should get our first awkward moment out of the way now—to make for smoother sailing on our first date.

Our *first date?* Did you ever get the feeling you'd gone just a little too far but were having *way* too much fun to bother caring? I could have signed off at any time, but instead I said ...

DoubleDee: And what, my dear Billy Boy, would this first date consist of?

As much as I wanted to claw Grace's skanky little eyes out, I almost wished she were with me right then, if only to catch me calling our Honors English teacher "my dear Billy Boy."

> Doctor_Love: Well, that, my sweet Fiji, would be up to you. I always let the woman lead . . . at least in the beginning.

**JAS88 has signed on**

*Whoa, my God!*

> **JAS88:** Hey.

Did he really expect me to answer him? After the totally heartless way he blew me off before?

> **JJ_Pearl:** Hey.

Okay, so I'm a sucker for guys who treat me like dog doody. Welcome to life as a teenage girl.

> **JAS88:** Sorry about before. My roommate was nagging me to get off the computer. We had a party to go to, but it was lame, so I'm back.
> **JJ_Pearl:** You could've said goodbye.

*You go, girl! Give him hell!*

**JAS88:** I know, sorry. But you sorta shocked me. How'd you get my screen name, anyway?

**JJ_Pearl:** Long story.

**JAS88:** Listen, don't be mad about what happened, okay?

**JJ_Pearl:** Between me and you, or between you and Grace?

**JAS88:** You're not gonna tell Alona, are you?

**JJ_Pearl:** What do you care?

**JAS88:** I just don't want her thinking I'm an asshole. There's an unwritten code every big brother's supposed to follow: *You don't fool around with your sister's friends.* It's that simple.

**JJ_Pearl:** Yeah, so simple you managed to screw up how many times?

**JAS88:** I didn't make you do anything you didn't want to do.

He had a point there.

**JAS88:** Grace either.

*Which reminds me . . .*

**JJ_Pearl:** And you and Grace have been getting together for how long?

★ ★ ★

Doctor_Love: Yoohoo, you still there? I thought we were supposed to be planning our first date.

*Crap. Mr. Fenowitz. I mean Doctor_Love. I mean Bill. I mean ...*

DoubleDee: Of course I'm still here. I was just looking for my shoe.

*Idiot.*

Doctor_Love: Oh, believe me. I understand all about women and shoes. I grew up in a house with three sisters. They're all married with kids now and can't understand why a smart, handsome "catch" like me is still single.
DoubleDee: Well, you *are* handsome.
Doctor_Love: Why, thank you. But what

makes you so sure—are you psychic?
Or . . . have we met and you're just not
telling me?

*Oops.* Screwed *that* one up. I guess I got lost in the
moment for a second, forgot I was acting. *Note to self:
Never get lost in the moment when you're busy cyberseduc-
ing one of your teachers, who just* happens *to think you're
a twenty-five-year-old sex goddess named Fiji. Not to mention when you're also web juggling two guys at once. Which
reminds me . . .*

**JJ_Pearl:** Earth to Jordan! I asked about you
and Grace.
**JAS88:** I know. Sorry. I was chatting with someone else.
**JJ_Pearl:** Your girlfriend?
**JAS88:** No, one of my old basketball buddies
from Beaubridge. And in answer to your question,
Grace and I haven't been "getting together." It
was one time. Same as you and me.

Well, hearing that was a relief. Sort of. At least if this
were a race, Grace wouldn't be winning. We'd be tied—
along with half the female population of Penn State.

**JJ_Pearl:** So, is that how you justify cheating? You get with all these other girls *one time* so that if the news ever traveled back to your girlfriend you could say it was just an isolated incident, a one-time fling that didn't mean anything?

**JAS88:** You know, you're pretty sharp for a kid.

**JJ_Pearl:** If I'm just a kid, why'd you hook up with me?

\* \* \*

Doctor_Love: Looking for your other lost shoe, I take it?

See? I really *am* an idiot. Why was I wasting my time talking to an obvious player when I could've been planning my romantic first date with . . . oh, right, my *English teacher.* You know, the older I get, the more I've come to realize that life is just one big, smelly pile of cow shit. And I'm constantly stepping in it.

DoubleDee: Sorry, I've gotta jam. My roommate's nagging me to get off the computer so we can go meet up with our friends.

Doctor_Love: Oh, that's too bad. For me,
I mean. But you have fun.
DoubleDee: I plan to, handsome. And the
answer is no, by the way—we haven't met.
I am a little bit psychic, though, but
only when it comes to sniffing out the
hotties. I guess you could say I have a
built-in stud detector.

*Huh?* What kind of freak was I turning into . . . and
why was I so damn good at it?

Doctor_Love: LOL. Well, before you go,
take down my e-mail, would you? It's
so refreshing to actually meet a normal
human being on one of these sites.
I'd really like it if we could stay
in touch.

He thinks *I'm* normal? Okay, this just in: We are *all*
going straight to hell.

After parting ways with older man number one—
who blew the cork off his not-so-secret identity by providing the e-mail address *bfenowitz@beaubridgehs.com*—I
turned my attention back to older man number two.

**JJ_Pearl:** I'm waiting . . .
**JAS88:** Sorry, what was the question?
**JAS88:** ☺
**JJ_Pearl:** Are you really that ignorant?
**JAS88:** Oh, come on, CG, don't be like that.

*He called me CG! He remembers my name! And damn well he should,* I reasoned, considering our little rendezvous was only eight days ago. I mean, sure, the guy's a bit of an asshole, but that's not an automatic excuse for early Alzheimer's.

**JJ_Pearl:** I had asked why you hooked up with me.
**JAS88:** Because you were there.

That couldn't possibly have been the real reason . . . *Could it have?* I mean, I know I said he was a jerk, but he's the hottest jerk who's ever had his hands on me.

**JAS88:** And I wanted to.

*Now* that's *more like it.* I smiled coyly, huddling closer to the monitor, even though my parents, safely tucked away in the downstairs den, couldn't possibly have observed what I was typing.

**JJ_Pearl:** I wanted to, too.

**JAS88:** So, then, what are we arguing about?

**JJ_Pearl:** We're not.

**JAS88:** Good. Because I like you, CG.

**JJ_Pearl:** I like you, too.

*Holy mother of Bill!* Was this really happening?

**JAS88:** You know I'll be home in six weeks for Easter. Maybe you'll be . . .

**JJ_Pearl:** Sleeping over that weekend?

**JAS88:** See that? Great minds really do think alike.

I couldn't wait to tell Glory about this. Of course, I'd have to exaggerate a little, taking into account the fact that she thinks Jordan and I are already together. But a good story always needs the right motivational spark, and there were enough sparks flying between Jordan and me during this little IM chat to ignite a forest fire. Maybe I'd make the story dirty, tell her about all the naughty things he was saying he wants to do to me when he comes home for Easter break. She'd buy it. Glory buys everything I tell her. The scary part is, I'm starting to feel a little guilty. Probably because I like the girl more than I ever intended to. We've even started hanging out and *not* talking about Jordan, like the other day when she came over to watch my grandmother's old VHS copy of *Woodstock* and laugh at all the naked hippies. Alex and I used to do shit like that together— things I couldn't imagine doing with the Four Tops in a million years.

> **JAS88:** Hey, listen, I've gotta go.

*So soon?*

> **JAS88:** But I'm glad we talked.
> **JJ_Pearl:** Yeah, me, too. And I've gotta go also. My friend Bill just signed on.

Hey, if there's one thing I've already learned from Jordan, it's how to play the game: Never let him think he's the only one. Always let him know there's someone else—someone even better, maybe—waiting in the wings.

> **JAS88:** Oh yeah?
> **JJ_Pearl:** Yup.
> **JAS88:** Who's Bill?

*See what I mean?*

\* \* \*

So, it's now been thirty-six hours since I officially de-
buted my juggling act, and here I am, back to being a
respectable fifteen-year-old honors student, sitting in
second period English class listening to the painfully
clumsy Charlie Packer bumble through his ten-page essay on *The Catcher in the Rye.* I've gotta tell you, though,
I'm finding it next to impossible to concentrate. I just
keep replaying Saturday night over and over in my mind,
remembering every word he wrote to me. But for some
inexplicable reason, it's not the *he* I thought it would be.

"And do we agree with Charlie's take on what Salin-
ger was trying to communicate in that second-to-last
chapter? Anyone?" Mr. Fenowitz asks as he peers curiously around the room. "CG, how about you? What's
your take on chapter twenty-five?"

I stare into his deep, soulful brown eyes and must
literally remind myself not to faint. "I'm sorry," I say,
smiling. "Can I have a nurse's pass? I think I need to go
lie down." Because I've just fallen head over heels.

# nine chewing the fat

"Do you want a snack?" I ask as Sammie shifts awkwardly about my living room, taking in her luxurious microscopic surroundings. I've never been to Sammie's house, but I can only assume it's as mansionesque as Alona's and Grace's. My place, on the other hand, could make the Old Lady's Shoe look like Caesars Palace. We had much bigger digs in the city, but you couldn't eat off the sidewalks there and the school system was going to hell on a motorbike. I guess that's what they mean when they say life is all about tradeoffs.

"No, nothing for me, thanks."

*What?* But that was part of my master plan: Get the girl to chow down so I can segue into the weight subject. Yes, I'm actually going through with this bullshit task. I gave Alona my word, didn't I? Not that my word is really worth much these days. I swear, I'm beginning to lose track of who I'm even supposed to be anymore. We're studying the world economy in history class, and yesterday Ms. Doyle mentioned that sugar was the main export of Fiji. I actually said, "What?" I thought she was talking to *me*.

So, Sammie doesn't want to eat, huh? I guess it's time to come up with a Plan B.

"Yeah," I say, flopping down onto our old burgundy-and-navy plaid couch. "I really shouldn't eat, either." I unzip my black hoodie, lifting up the fitted gray T-shirt I've got on underneath to expose my tummy roll. I mean, face it, this is Beaubridge, not LA. With the exception of Alona and Grace, who *doesn't* have their own personal bakery going on when they sit down?

"What are *you* talking about?" Sammie asks in that low, gravelly voice of hers. "I would, like, *kill* for your body."

See, I'm really not the one to be helping Sammie out with this sort of thing because, personally, I've never understood it. I mean, if you're gonna *kill* for something, why not make it for a rare Janis Joplin recording or eternal celebrity status at your school—complete and utter immunity from ever being deemed a nobody by the likes of this world's Alona Speltons—you know, important stuff like that?

"Please," I say. "My body's far from perfect."

"Well, it's more perfect than mine," she says, sitting down beside me. "*Way* more perfect."

"Why do you say that?" This is good. Get her talking about those pesky figure flaws Alona is so obsessed with, and we'll figure out how to change them. Then I can get my gold star for the day, and everyone's a winner.

"Have you *seen* me next to the three of you?" she asks. "I look like the Jolly Green Giant."

*Uh, make that the Jolly Orange Giant.*

"No, you don't!" I blurt instinctively. I mean, that's only normal, right? To contradict someone after they've just said something completely hideous and demeaning about themselves? Even if it is kind of true. Okay, totally true. "I would, like, *kill* to be as tall as you," I say, stealing her phraseology. And lying at the same time. Then again, that whole skyscraper thing has worked for Heidi Klum. "You could grow up to be on *America's Next Top Model* or something. Alona, Grace, and I would never have that option." Sweet mother of God, I genuinely suck at this. I'm supposed to be cutting her *down,* not pumping her up.

Sammie smiles momentarily, but her happy face is quickly overshadowed by a look of doom. "I could never be a model. My thighs are too big."

"Well, have you ever tried running? That seems like a good way to lose some weight." Aha! It took a little while, but here we go—treading down the exact path our precious leader was hoping for. Oh, if Alona could see me now.

"I've tried *everything*."

"Oh." Well, so much for *that* brilliant idea.

"And nothing seems to work."

*"Nothing?"*

She nods, her dark eyes filling up with sadness. "There have been times when I've exercised for hours, and still . . . nothing. I just don't think I was meant to be skinny."

"Well, you're not *fat,* Sammie. You're just—"

"I know, I know. Big boned, curvy, stout, built like a linebacker—even though I'm not the slightest bit athletic."

Well, that just about covers it.

"So, what do all those teen magazines keep telling us?" I ask her. "And our health and phys ed teachers, too?"

Sammie shrugs. "You've got me."

"That we should embrace our bodies the way they are. And to hell with Nicole Richie and Mary-Kate Olsen—"

"And Alona Spelton," Sammie adds, smiling.

We both laugh, and I think it's the first time Sammie and I have ever "gotten" each other. Hell, I think it's the first time Sammie has ever gotten *anything.* But the sheer mention of Alona's name reminds me all too well of our deal. She's gonna expect a full report, and what am I supposed to tell her? That Sammie is simply unshrinkable?

"What about your diet?" I ask, changing my tone.

Sammie appears confused. "But I thought you said—"

"Well, it never hurts to eat right."

"I eat right," Sammie says, flopping against the back of the couch. She lets out a little sigh of defeat. "I just eat too much."

"Well, maybe if you drank a glass of water before each meal, you'd be less hungry."

She turns to stare at me, her eyes bulging forth from their sockets as if I've got the word *dunce* smeared across my forehead in poop. "I don't eat because I'm hungry."

"Well, then . . . why *do* you eat?"

*Ding-dong!* Saved by the doorbell, a clearly ticked-off Sammie takes to studying her fire engine red fingernails while I get up to see who it is.

Uh, can you say *crapola?* With a double shot of shit and a twist? It's *Glory!* And to make matters worse, she's wearing the overalls today—with an actual *handkerchief* sticking out of the front chest pocket. I can see the entire ensemble peeking out from beneath her unzipped parka like an embarrassing secret she's not quite ready to share with the world. Sort of like what she is to me. I mean, sure, the gang knows I talk to her—in a neigh-borly, *Was that* your *mother's rose garden my dog fertilized last night?* kind of way—but they have no idea she's be-come a real friend with certified hangout privileges. How in God's name am I gonna play this off in front of Sammie?

"Hey," I say to Glory, opening the door. "Um, I'm kind of tied up right now. Did we have plans?"

"Noooo," Glory says brightly, sidestepping me into the foyer. "But you promised to tell me all about your online affair with that thirty-year-old. And you weren't on the bus home from school today, so I decided to come by and get the scoop. What are you tied up with?"

Okay, pause it. I need to give you a little background. For one, the friendlier I've gotten with Glory, the faster she talks. But I kind of like it. Between that, her Carrot Top hairdo, and farmer fashion sense, she certainly is an eccentric character. Secondly, "that thirty-year-old" is actually twenty-nine-year-old Mr. Fenowitz. I don't know why I felt compelled to round up. I guess thirty just sounds so much older than twenty-nine and, for that reason, so much racier, therefore making fifteen-year-old me sound all the more rebellious for taking the plunge with him. Not that there's been any actual plunging go-ing on. I've been too chicken to e-mail Mr. Fenowitz—I mean Bill—since he gave me his address four days ago,

but I have been chatting with Jordan, who I still fantasize about hooking up with come Easter. It's just that
he's no Doctor Love. Bill knows how to make a woman
feel special and warm and one of a kind. And come on,
ladies, who wouldn't want that? Oh, but back to this
whole Glory–Sammie thing . . .

"I wasn't on the bus because I got a ride home," I
tell Glory. "But, um, don't ever say anything in front
of my parents because the person doesn't have their license yet."

"You went driving without a license!" Glory shouts.
"You really are my little rebel!"

"Ssh," I whisper, trying to quiet her. "It's not as if *I*
was the one driving, and besides, she's planning on going
for her permit any day now."

"She who?" Glory asks, taking a step backward
toward the door.

And as if that were her cue, Sammie enters the foyer
in her ill-fitting turquoise mini and Uggs. "Hey, Ceej,
where's your bathroom?" Upon noticing Glory, whose
ivory complexion has suddenly turned a deep shade of
pink, she does nothing to acknowledge her presence.

"Hello, Samara," Glory sputters, taking yet another
step toward the door.

I take hold of Glory's arm, drawing her closer. I mean,
come on, people, we all know geek and chic don't mix,

but we're not exactly talking Hussein versus Bush, here. For shit's sake, this is *high school.*

"Glory was just stopping by to borrow a cup of sugar," I say pointedly, aiming to let my clumsy confidante know that Sammie isn't privy to my recent online escapades with a certain much-older man. Though when I think about it . . . *a cup of sugar?* What are we, forty? "But . . ." And here goes the plunge of the century. "I've invited her to stay and hang out with us."

*"What?"* my two friends ask in unison, both equally dismayed. Alona was right: I am one ballsy chick. If I do say so myself.

"Sammie, the bathroom's upstairs, first door on your left. You'll recognize it by the toilet. And you," I say, turning to Glory, "do you need that sugar right away, or do you think you could chill a little while?"

She smiles gratefully, and for a second, I have the irresistible urge to reach out and squeeze the juice out of those innocent little apple cheeks of hers. Flushed as they still are. "I can chill."

"Fabulous," I say as a confused-as-ever Sammie heads for the stairs. Once she's disappeared, I pull Glory into the kitchen and, using my most efficient "library voice," attempt to explain my current dilemma.

"So, wait," Glory whispers when I'm finished. "You

brought Samara over today because Alona asked you to tell her she's big?"

"Basically."

"Well, you can't *tell* somebody that!"

"Too late. She already knows."

"Of *course* she knows," Glory says, flailing her animated hands in the air. "But you can't *talk* about it. The whole time I was friends with her we *never* talked about it. *She* talked about it. I just, you know, listened. And then there was Grace, who called her Sasquatch."

I let out an involuntary gasp. "Not to her face, I hope."

Glory gives me a doubtful look. "Have you *met* Grace Checkov?"

I shake my head. "Who would treat someone that way?"

Glory shrugs. "She thought it was funny. Apparently, Samara didn't agree."

"So, she stopped saying it, then?" I ask, taking a quick peek out into the living room to make sure the coast is still clear. "Once she realized how much it bothered Sammie?"

"Like I said, have you met Grace Checkov?"

I lean back against the refrigerator and sigh. "What a—"

"Careful there. She happens to be one of your best friends, remember?"

"Every day of my life," I say through gritted teeth.

Glory laughs. "Yeah, well, don't complain, then. Most girls at Beaubridge would do just about anything to walk a mile in your shoes." Suddenly, her whole face brightens. "That's it!" she exclaims, as if someone just turned on the light switch in her brain.

"What's it?" I whisper. "And be quiet."

"We'll go for a walk," she says, lowering her voice. "You, me, and Samara. If we make it seem like a fun little afterschool activity, she won't think of it as exercise. Then, she won't set herself up to fail—since she's claimed to have tried *everything*—and you will have done your good deed for Alona. Who knows? It could even become a regular thing, and she may even lose some weight."

"Hold your fire. Since when did taking a walk in the armpit of suburbia on a freezing February afternoon become a fun activity?"

Glory laughs quietly. "Since I said so."

"It's thirty-one freaking degrees out there!" I nearly scream.

"So, that only means we'll walk faster. And the faster you walk—"

"The more calories you burn," Sammie concludes, joining us in the kitchen.

Holy thighs of thunder, I never even heard her coming!

"Oh, hey," I say, trying not to sound as stunned as I feel. "Glory was just suggesting we go for a walk. But I told her—"

"That it's thirty-one freaking degrees out there." Sammie smiles. "I know. I heard." *Uh, please tell me that's all you heard.* She turns to Glory. "So, how've you been?"

"Me?" Glory asks shyly as she backs into one of my kitchen chairs, which grates awkwardly against the linoleum floor, echoing her bumbling uncertainty.

"Easy there, killer," I tease, placing my hands upon her fragile, nervous shoulders. This seems to steady her, and we all break into laughter. It truly feels as if the ice has been broken. And speaking of ice . . .

"I don't care how frosty it is out there. I'll walk if you guys are up for it," Sammie says.

Glory smiles at her, and I realize this is the closest she's come to having her friend back in almost two years. "Sounds good to me."

"Okay, fine," I say. "Twist my arm. I'll go get my jacket."

Sammie follows me to the coat closet as Glory moves toward the front door, zipping up her parka.

"Hey, Ceej, I was thinking," Sammie whispers as we bundle up. "Maybe we could keep this thing about

hanging out with Glory just between the two of us—
like not say anything to Alona and Grace about it?"

I take a moment to act as if I'm considering her
proposition, weighing the pros and cons, debating the
morality conflicts, searching my soul . . . "Sure," I say finally. "Why not? I guess it wouldn't kill me to keep *one*
harmless little secret."

# ten keeping up with the crumpets

"Wait just one second," Grace says as she rifles through the overpriced dress rack at Blake's Boutique. It's Saturday afternoon, and the four of us—make that the three of *them*—are taking advantage of the early spring "sales." She turns to face me, her sneaky hazel eyes twinkling with suspicion. "You're trying to tell us you've been having an Internet affair with Mr. F?"

"I'm not *trying* to tell you," I say, casually taking a seat on one of the cushy vinyl benches by the dressing rooms. "I *am* telling you."

Alona giggles and reaches down to tousle my bangs. "I love you, CG. You're such a little lawbreaker."

"No, actually, *he's* the lawbreaker," Grace snarls. "I mean, what kind of freakazoid perv would go stalking women half his age over the Internet?" She shudders over-dramatically and waltzes off into an open dressing room

"Well, he doesn't *know* she's fifteen," Alona points out.

"And besides, I thought you had a crush on that 'freakazoid perv,'" Sammie adds. The three of us simultaneously bite our lower lips in dreaded anticipation of the she-devil's poisonous response. But there is none.

"Uh, Grace? Sammie was just teasing," Alona says sweetly.

"Whatever," my nemesis calls from behind her closed door.

And *this* is why I decided to tell them about Bill and me. Because I knew it would drive Grace up the mother-effing wall. Well, this and the fact that I can't stop thinking about him. Especially since we started e-mailing. That's right, I actually went through with it, made up a dummy Hotmail account and wrote him the night I got home from my little power walk with Glory and Sammie. You know, the walk that never happened.

"So, how many times have you two e-mailed?" Alona asks, joining me on the pink vinyl bench, which coincidentally matches her snakeskin cowboy boots and the giant "Bennifer" rock she's wearing on her right hand. Holy Moses, this girl has got her shit together.

"Um, every day since Wednesday."

"Is that all?" Grace asks, suddenly reappearing in a glittery gold halter dress that positively screams *Put me back!* She goes to check herself out in one of the boutique's three-way mirrors. "You made it seem as if you guys were already talking marriage." She turns to face us. "What do you think?"

"I think you look like a lost Supreme," I tell her. "Only this isn't 1967."

A stunned silence fills the store until Sammie begins to giggle—quietly at first, then increasingly louder until her chuckling becomes a runaway laugh track she can't even attempt to conceal. I'm not sure if it was hanging out alone with me, or "not hanging out" with Glory and me, but whatever the cause, Sammie's been more expressive these last few days. More willing to say what's on her mind. And let's face it, up until now, who knew she ever even *had* anything on her mind?

"Yeah, it's real funny, isn't it, Sasquatch?" Grace snaps, stomping back off toward the dressing room.

"Hey!" I shout, standing up to go after her.

"Don't," Alona says softly, putting her hand on my arm to restrain me. "Just let her cool down." She bats her big baby blues and smiles pleadingly. "I can't stand it when my friends fight. And besides . . ." She lowers her voice to a whisper. "You know she's just jealous of you."

Um, can you say *music to my precious eardrums?* I know I shouldn't hate Grace anymore since I'm technically no longer obsessed with Jordan, but can I help it if everything she says just irks the crap out of me? Or if the sheer thought of her and Jordan hooking up still makes my skin crawl like a gazillion rattlesnakes with fleas? I mean, I'm sure you've heard the expression about having your cake and eating it, too. Well, right now Bill is my cake, but Jordan's the sweet-baked hunk of delicious I plan on digging into over Easter break. And the thought of sinking my teeth through anything Grace has already salivated over makes me want to toss my cookies. Enough sugary snack metaphors for one paragraph? I thought so.

"You really think she's jealous?" I whisper back to Alona.

She gives me an affirmative nod. "Totes." That's Alona speak for "totally." Yet another one of her worthy causes. Why save the rainforest, the whales, or the world when you can devote your time to saving *syllables?* "By the way," she says, turning to Sammie, "what's a Sasquatch?"

* * *

"Honey, did you want some more tuna casserole?" my mom asks, the spatula already poised in her hand.

I shrug, forking over my plate. The truth is, I'm not even remotely hungry tonight. The butterflies in my belly are too busy counting down the minutes 'til this meal is over to bother with anything as mundane as eating. I mean, who can concentrate on food when they've got a date with destiny? Okay, so it's not exactly a *date,* but I am planning on taking over my dad's PC later in hopes of another Saturday night rendezvous with my favorite naughty professor.

"And you've barely touched your mashed potatoes," my mom observes as I attempt to make nice with the milky mound of fish noodles she's just plopped in front of me.

"Oh, come on, Rosie," my father says with a little wink. "You can't expect her to get turned on by tuna casserole and mashed potatoes anymore, not now that she's been exposed to a life of caviar and crumpets."

"Okay, first of all," I say, rolling my eyes, "I was never 'turned on' by mom's cooking. No offense," I add, turning to her. "And secondly, my friends aren't as spoiled as you guys make them seem." Actually, they're worse, but I'd never give my dad the satisfaction of knowing his assessments were accurate. Especially when he's trying to be funny. I mean, I love my dad and everything, but you know how it is when your parents use your life as a launching pad for their latest comedy routines. Not exactly a laugh riot.

"Of *course* they're not," my mom says, joining in on

the act with a sarcastically raised brow. "By the way, how was shopping today at Blake's Boutique? I think I saw a scarf on sale there last week for nine thousand dollars."

"Aw, you should've gotten it," I say, playing along. "It would've gone so nicely with that stylish sweatsuit you bought at Target the week before." I stop to smile, remembering the way I razzed her when she tried it on in the dressing room, teasing that all the other neighborhood moms would be jealous once they got a load of her sexy tapered elastic-ankle pants. "You know, the one with the really cool bottoms." Now, *that* was funny. I can tell because my dad nearly choked on his green beans.

"Make fun of me all you want," my mom says, feigning hurt feelings. Even though she secretly lives for this shit. She told me just the other day how stoked she is that we can still joke about things. And I guess I'm pretty stoked, too—especially when the joke's on her. It would suck balls to have parents I couldn't have any fun with. "One day, you'll be just like me," she continues, "when you're old enough to realize that it really doesn't matter how you look."

"I think she realized that a long time ago," my dad says, stifling a laugh as he tugs on my oversized hoodie. "The fashion editors at *Vogue* haven't exactly been pounding her door down either."

"Well, they *would* be," I say, chugging back a swig of iced tea, "if you guys would just cough up your life's savings already so I could go shopping with my friends."

To this, we all giggle. And I'm glad. I'd never actually want my parents to feel bad about the things they can't afford to give me, most of which I have no interest in anyway. They know I wouldn't be able to tell real cashmere from a soft clump of fur on a cat's ass, but it's still nice to remind them every once in a while—in case they're worried I might one day have the urge to splurge and try maxing out their credit cards at the latest overpriced, *even the* salesgirl's *shit don't stink* boutique.

"Speaking of my friends," I say, preparing for my escape to Billville, "we're planning another Saturday night rap session online. Is it okay if I use the computer?"

"Only if you finish your tuna casserole," my mom insists. And this time she isn't kidding. Mothers never joke about dinner.

"You've got a deal," I tell her. And suddenly, Mom's milky mound of fish noodles never tasted so good. I snort that shit back like it's crack and bolt upstairs to my dad's office for "dessert" (if you perverts know what I mean).

# eleven extra credit

Monday mornings. Glorious, notorious Monday mornings. I used to dread them—hell, I used to dread Tuesday through Friday mornings, too—but that was before I started living for second period. Bill is handing back our bluebook essays today. I know I just wowed him with my analysis on the loss of innocence in *The Catcher in the Rye. Come on, Billy Boy,* I think as he walks about the room, holding each of our fates in his strong, capable hands. *Come to Mama. Bring me my A-plus.*

"*D-minus?*" I shriek upon opening my exam. A few heads turn to stare at me, but I don't care. I'm too ... I can't even find the word to describe it—that's how *too* I am. I mean, how could he *do* this to me? I really thought we had something.

"*You know I've never met a woman like you before,*" he wrote just last night in his fifth e-mail to me. This following a late-night chat session on Saturday that lasted for nearly three whole hours. *"It's so refreshing to meet someone I can just be myself around."* Does being himself mean handing out near-failing grades? What a . . .

"Bastard!"

Bill whips around and stares at me, stunned. His sexy, soulful brown eyes have suddenly turned a frightening shade of "teacher." It seems in the last week or so, I've forgotten that in addition to *stone cold fox,* this man's also got the words *authority figure* written all over him. Shit, I could get *expelled* for what I just said. On one hand, that could take this whole rebel thing to brand-new heights, but on the other . . . you've never seen my father angry.

"I'm sorry?" Bill asks.

"Oh no," I stammer, laughing clumsily. "Not *you.* I was just, um . . . practicing my Tourette's."

Now it's the class's turn to laugh. In fact, I think I even see my dearly beloved cracking a little smile.

"Come again?" he asks.

"I'm, um, trying out for this play in New York on Saturday and the role I'm auditioning for is a young girl with Tourette's syndrome. You know that thing where people go around shouting obscenities and can't control their bodily tics."

"I'm well aware of what Tourette's syndrome is, CG,"

Bill says dryly. "My sister Gabrielle has been grappling with the disorder since we were kids."

Have you ever wished you could bury your head in your own ass just to avoid having people see the shame on your face? Uh, *yeah.* This is definitely one of those contortionist moments. But, wait, what's with that little glint in Bill's eye?

He leans down and whispers softly in my ear, "Gotcha."

The class remains oblivious, and—remembering his previous prank about his father's "car crash" and how he ended up with the boring name Bill—I'm the only one who laughs. Who knew my future hubby was such a sophisticated jokester?

"Anyway," he says, straightening up, "see me after class." *With pleasure, baby.* "And we'll see if we can't think of a way to raise your grade." *I can think of one way.*

"Sounds good to me. And, um . . . thanks."

★ ★ ★

So, here we are. After class. Just me and my man. And a room about to fill up with students.

"You wanted to see me?" I ask.

"Right. I wanted to talk to you about your test. I've gotta say I was pretty shocked by this one, CG. Up until now, you've been doing so well." Bill scratches his head, peering at me in that guidance counselor, *Is there something going on I should know about?* sort of way that would normally inspire an eye roll of massive proportions. Only I can tell that he genuinely cares about me. Which is why I decide to whip out the tears.

"I know I've been doing well!" I blurt, wiping my eyes, which, I've gotta admit, are still as dry as the Sahara. I mean, hey, I'm no Meryl Streep, here. But where there's a will, there's a . . .

"Ahaaaaaaaa!" I wail, stabbing my palm against the jar full of freshly sharpened pencil points on Bill's desk. And this time, I assure you, my tears are real.

Bill immediately grabs for my hand. I knew this relationship would eventually get physical. *Now just kiss me, you fool.* "My *God,* are you okay?" he asks.

"No!" I cry. "I mean, yes." Actually, I'm not. My hand is stinging like a mother. But it's all in the name of love. And literature. "It's just that I expected to do really well on this essay, and I can't believe I blew it!"

"Yeah, but, CG," he says, still holding my hand, "that's no reason for self-mutilation." He pauses for a second, giving me that guidance counselor look again. "Have you ever done this kind of thing before?"

Oh, boy. Here we go. The mandatory life-lesson monologue, ripped straight from the pages of the *How to Talk to Teens Handbook.* God, I hate that handbook.

"Because if you have," he continues, "you need to know that hurting yourself is never a viable solution to any problem." *Still holding my hand.* "And what may seem like an earth-shattering crisis to you now won't even be a blip in your memory bank a year from now. Because youth . . . It's like an express train—there are always new surprises waiting for you just around the bend." *Well, how about climbing aboard, then? Because I'm more than willing to share the ride.* "What I'm saying is, one bad grade on a bluebook essay test isn't the end of the world, and if you're feeling this bad about it, so bad that you want to hurt yourself—"

"I don't," I say, cutting him off. *Sheesh.* I mean, being comforted is one thing. Having the man of my dreams think I'm some sort of suicide case is clearly another. "It was an accident. Really. I'm just a complete spaz some-times, that's all. And when the arms start flailing, look out—you never know *what* can happen."

He smiles, laughing gently. Oh, and did I mention that he's *still* holding my hand? "Well, as long as I don't have to go to bed tonight worrying about you."

"No," I say sweetly. "You don't have to." *But you could if you* want *to . . . think about me in bed, I mean.*

"All right, then," he says, finally letting go of my poor, throbbing hand. I glance down at my palm, which, as I dreadfully suspected, is swollen, purple, and full of tiny black dots. "I'll write you a nurse's pass for that. But first, I have a proposition for you."

"Oh yeah?" *Anything, my dear Billy boy. Just say the word and I'm yours!*

"I'm going to need a couple of students to help me prepare study guides for next year's freshman reading list. Now, you'd get extra credit for this, which would help improve your average after that D-minus, but it would require spending some time with me after school—"

"Done!" I exclaim. Whoops. I guess if Overeager had a retarded cousin, it would definitely be me. Fortunately, Bill mistakes my infatuation for academic enthusiasm.

"Well, great. We'll get started next week. I'll give you more details tomorrow."

"Super." *Super?* Who *says* that?

Bill writes out my nurse's pass, and as I turn to leave the room I see his entire third-period class sitting there facing me, all of them politely trying not to gawk at the tear-streaked face of a lovesick fool who's just made plans with fate. Well, make that all except *one*.

"Hey, Silverman," Grace says brashly, grabbing me by the elbow, "why was Mr. F holding your hand?"

I shrug her off and keep walking. "Wouldn't *you* like to know."

# twelve the apprentice

Okay, so remind me why I agreed to do this. As I sit here surrounded by piles—no, make that *mountains*—of literary nonsense, trying to figure out how to translate thousands of pages of yakety-yak into seven coherent sets of study questions, I can't help but notice that my darling Bill is nowhere to be found. This is supposed to be our time together. And I'm *supposed* to be getting help. Bill said he needed a *couple* of students to work on this project. So far all I see is ...

"*Grace?*" What is *she* doing here? "What are *you* doing here?"

"Mr. F asked me to help him out for extra credit," she explains aloofly, strutting her stuff across the room. She lifts herself up onto his desk—*his desk?*—and crosses her legs, seductively dangling one of her Manolos off her right foot. I could never pull that off. Not that I'd actually want to. I mean, do *you* know how to say *cheesy* in fifteen different languages?

"But you don't need extra credit," I point out. "You got a B-plus on your last exam."

"Yeah, well," she says loftily, studying her shiny violet fingernails, "I'm an *A-plus* kind of woman."

"Really?" I ask, my tone as snide as I can possibly make it. "That's not what I hear."

"That's not what you hear from whom?"

"Oh, no one. Just a little birdie." *A little birdie named Jordan Spelton who says you kiss like a dead fish. He also says you're an annoying ho who occasionally still stalks him online. He's thinking of getting a restraining order.*

"A little *birdie,* CG?" she asks incredulously. "Nobody talks like that. Who are you, Rebecca of Sunnybrook Farm?"

"You've read *Rebecca of Sunnybrook Farm*?" a familiar voice asks from the doorway. "Somehow I didn't have you pegged as a fan of classic children's lit."

We both turn around suddenly. "Mr. Fenowitz!" Our singsong harmony makes me want to spew.

"The one and only," he says with a charming smile. "Sorry I'm late." He glances over at me. "Good, CG, I see you've found my secret stash."

"Your what–what who?" I stammer, still dizzy from his entrance.

Bill laughs and gives a little nod toward the overflow-ing mound of books on my desk.

"Oh, right." *Der.* I pick up a copy of both *To Kill a Mockingbird* and *Inherit the Wind* to show him that I know what books are. "These."

"She found them, but she won't share," Grace whines, pouting as she folds her arms across her overly accentu-ated mosquito bites. Ever hear of "The bigger the better, the tighter the sweater"? Well, Grace may have the tight sweater part down, but making honkers out of *those* little niblets would definitely be a chore for the Baby Gap. Which might explain where she got that *skirt.* Forever Skankalicious must've been closed yesterday.

"Oh, come on, Grace," Bill says. "You've never had a problem asserting yourself before. Just march on over there and split the stack. And while you're at it, you may find you're more comfortable sitting in a *chair.*" He smiles sheepishly, his boyish dimples making sweet little pock-ets on either side of his grin. "Besides, haven't you ever heard the expression 'Tables are for glasses, not asses'?"

The three of us laugh over my so-called friend's bla-tantly failed seduction attempt (did she really think she'd win him over by smothering his paperwork in her butt cheeks?), but I can tell Grace is only laughing on the outside—she doesn't find Bill's diss even remotely amus-ing. *I* sure as hell do, though. I mean, a teacher saying *ass* is always a crowd pleaser, no matter which way you slice it. Compound that with Grace's humiliation, and I'll be pissing my Hanes for a week.

On her way over to my desk, Grace drops her pencil. Accidentally on purpose, of course. *Oy vey.* You know the drill from here. In *Legally Blonde,* Reese Witherspoon called it the "Bend and Snap." In Grace's case, I call it the "I See London." Because she's clearly aiming to provide Bill—and me in the unfortunate process—with a glimpse of what comes after France. Only this "A-plus woman" isn't wearing any underpants. Now, that's what I call *nasty,* with a capital N *and* an exclamation point!

"Grace," I whisper, yanking her arm until I manage to jerk her upright. "What are you doing?"

Bill, red as a candy apple, makes his way over to his desk. "Ladies, I've got some work to do," he says, his voice saturated with awkward formality. *Way to go, Grace. Does your ass have that effect on every guy you like? Or just the ones I like, too?* "If you two want to collaborate on this, that's fine. Just move to the back of the room, if you don't mind, so that I can still have some quiet."

"No, it's okay," Grace snaps. "I'm through talking to *her.*"

"Yeah, that's what you think," I mumble, linking elbows with the pantyless twit as I hurry—make that *drag*—her out of the room. Once we've gotten about halfway down the hall, I let loose on her. "What the hell do you think you're doing?"

"Ooh," she snarls. "Did somebody say the h-word? You must really be angry."

"Why are you trying to hit on Bill?"

*"Bill?"* she scoffs.

Oops. Force of habit. Glad the habit's never actually forced itself out in his presence. Like an accidental fart during jumping jacks or yoga or something.

"Sorry. Mr. Fenowitz," I say, correcting myself.

Grace smiles arrogantly as if I'm just some stupid kid in love. Which maybe I am. But that doesn't give her the right to smirk that way. If she does it again, I'm gonna pry her mouth open with a crowbar and take a dump in it.

"For your information," she says, "I wasn't the one doing the flirting. He was the one fawning over how assertive I am and making suggestive little comments about my ass."

I lurch forward as if I'm about to choke her to death—and for a second, I seriously consider it. Then, I just start yelling. "Have you completely lost your mind? He wasn't flirting with you!"

"Well, he wasn't flirting with *you*."

"I never said he was! But if he was gonna flirt with anyone, he would sure as hell choose me over some—"

"Some what?" she asks, popping her chin like a street hoodlum about to engage in a gang fight. "You want to finish that sentence?"

"Okay," I say with a casual shrug, hoping my blasé attitude might be enough to take the curl out of her hair. "Some cheap Alona Spelton rip-off who secretly . . ." Um, on second thought, maybe I shouldn't go there.

"Who secretly what?" she presses, jabbing my shoulder with one of her violet-colored claws. *Oh, screw it.* You may not be able to see them, but CG Silverman's got claws, too. And now that the gloves are off, I'm ready to draw blood.

"Who secretly wishes she was me."

The shoes on my feet: $13.95. My Salvation Army knapsack: a buck fifty. The look on Grace's face when I dragged *that* skeleton out of her closet: priceless. There are some things money can't buy. For everything else, there's my big brass balls.

"And what makes you think that?" Grace asks, her superior tone shrinking away.

"Well, how about the fact that until I came along, you were the smart one?"

"I'm *still* the smart one," she protests, "Ms. *D-minus.*" I guess screwing with Grace's confidence is like trying to dropkick that damn Energizer Bunny. No matter how hard you fight, they both just keep going and going . . .

"Yeah, and why do you think I got that D-minus?" I ask, determined to destroy her again.

Grace shrugs flippantly, making a sarcastic face. "Because you're an ignoramus?"

"Because I spent the whole night before the test chatting with Bill instead of studying, which brings me to reason number two: You can't stand that I got the guy and you didn't."

"You didn't *get* the guy, CG. He thinks you're ten years older than you really are and doesn't even know your real name. If you want the truth, I'd hardly call that 'getting the guy.' In fact, 'Bill' has a right to know you've been messing with him. I *think,*" she says, starting to walk past me, "that I'm going to march back in there and tell him exactly what's been going on."

"Don't you dare!" I scream, grabbing her by the back of the sweater, which makes a startling ripping sound as the fabric stretches between us.

"Let go," she hisses. "That's cashmere, you asshole."

"Don't you wanna hear reason number three?" Ignoring the malevolent flash in Grace's eyes, I continue. "Before I came along, you were the rebel of this group, and now nobody's impressed by anything you say or do anymore. Because your idea of being rebellious is being a mean-spirited witch, and if *you* want the truth, nobody thinks it's cool or funny or even the slightest bit cute."

"Oh, but you *are* all those things?" she barks, struggling to break free from my sweater lock.

"Alona and Sammie seem to think so, now don't they? Not that you give a rat's ass what Sammie thinks, but for some reason, you *are* starstruck by Alona."

"And you're not?"

"Of course I am. Everybody is. The only difference between me and everybody else—*you* being just like everybody else—is that Alona's also starstruck by me. And that, dear Gracie, is reason number four."

I've gotta admit, I *do* have the gift of gab. Judging by the look on Grace's face, I'd say I nailed her with that one final twist of the knife—or what shall forever be referred to as "The Alona Bomb." I watch as her jaw drops to the floor—we're talking full tonsil shot—and then she leans forward, so close I can almost taste her stale Cinnamint Orbit gum. Uh . . . is she gonna kiss me or kill me?

"I'm going to *bury* you."

Well, at least she settled *that* mystery.

"Not so fast," I warn her, yanking on that skanky overpriced sweater again. "If you blow my cover with Bill, I'll run and tell Alona all about your dirty little fling with her brother." Not that one dead-fish kiss is really much to write home about, but, hey, a threat is a threat. "You know, I've seen the way you and Sammie joke about your innocent schoolgirl crushes on Mr. Penn State. Good cover. Because yours really isn't so innocent, now, is it?"

The clump of cashmere in my fist grows tougher to grasp as Grace's body becomes one giant maraca, shaking to the beat of her own nerves. Good God, is she really *that* terrified of Alona? "How did you find out? What you're referring to isn't exactly public information."

"Yeah, I pretty much figured. Alona gets sort of freaked at the thought of that kind of thing."

"So, then . . . Jordan told you?"

Shit. *Note to self: When hanging people out to dry, be careful not to tie your own noose in the process.*

"Uh . . ."

"That night in his room. You weren't talking about his Victoria's Secret pictures, were you? You were talking about me."

"That's right!" I say thankfully. "The *one* time I ever talked to Jordan, he mentioned what went on with the two of you, told me everything."

"And that's *all* that happened?" she asks, raising her eyebrows suspiciously. "Because I'm not an idiot. I know how Jordan operates. He always gets what he's after. Of course, when we first gave you that silly little dare, I figured he'd just laugh you out the door, but the fact that he didn't means something else must've happened."

Now *I'm* the one shaking like a Latin American percussion instrument. "Well, even if that had been the case . . ." I fumble. "I mean, even if he *had* been after me, who's to say I would have gone along with it? Why wouldn't I have just said no?"

Grace stares at me blankly. "Because he's Jordan Spelton, and every girl wants him, that's why." Like, *duh*.

"And I'm CG Silverman," I say, thinking fast, "and I don't like to keep secrets from my friends. Which reminds me: Jordan says you can't kiss worth a damn and you had better quit stalking him online or he's gonna have to change his screen name and go into the witness protection program just to get away from your sorry, skeezy ass."

Are those tears I see welling up in her venomous hazel eyes? Okay, now I feel bad. Leave it to me to always take things just one measly little step too far.

"He really said that?" she asks softly.

"Um, maybe not in so many words. But seriously, maybe you *should* chill a little. I mean, there's no need to go all psycho over some guy you only made out with once."

"Is that what he told you?" she asks, eyeing me warily. I nod, shrugging, as Grace slips into her beggar's rags. "Listen," she says, her voice humble and pleading, "*please* don't say anything to Alona. I know you don't like to keep secrets, but what happened between Jordan and me was a mistake—I mean, obviously, if he said all that."

"Don't worry about it," I tell her. "I don't see any reason to upset Alona with this. But that means you have to keep your trap shut, too. About Bill and me."

"Well . . ." She pretends to hesitate for a moment, then smiles. "Okay." Does this mean we've called a truce? "Could you let go of my sweater now?"

"That would probably be a good idea, CG," says (*mother of shit!*) Bill, who has just come strolling down the hallway in search of his favorite little helpers. "You're both gonna need two hands to deal with the massive heap of toil that's waiting for you back in the room."

We both giggle nervously as I release my grip on Grace, whose flimsy body suddenly goes careening into thin air, nearly collapsing right into the arms of the man I love. Um, could we be any more dramatic?

"Listen, is everything okay?" Bill asks, his eyes shifting curiously between our two flustered faces. "I heard yelling and wanted to make sure my devoted apprentices weren't out here tearing each other's limbs off." He smiles. "This isn't a competition, you know. There's plenty of extra credit to go around."

"Oh, we know that," Grace says, showing him her best pageant beam. "CG and I are *never* competitive. Are we, Ceej?"

"Oh, never *ever*," I say, slinging my arm around her waist to demonstrate our harmonious rapport. "We're, like, the best of friends—two peas in a pod."

"Well, do me a favor and get your pod back to class before I find two other peas who are actually willing to *work* for their extra credit."

Yes, *sir*. God, I just love it when he gets saucy.

# thirteen just like old times

"How'd your extra credit thingie go?" Glory asks as we cross the dimly lit street. *We* being Glory, Sammie, and me—the new Three Musketeers (minus the very un-Musketeerish fact that the trio we've forged remains a dark, humiliating secret for at least two of us).

"It wasn't too bad," I say, refusing to delve into the Grace factor. I've been through enough with her nasty ass today. The last thing I want is to discuss that beast on my off-hours.

"You guys, I like walking when it's dark out like this," Sammie notes.

*Why? Because the undercover backdrop offers less risk of our being seen with the class leper?* Okay, that was mean. But at least I didn't say it out loud.

"Well, we could've taken our walk earlier," Glory

points out, "if *someone* wasn't so obsessed with sucking up to her favorite teacher."

"Ooh, *sucking* up?" Sammie repeats, a naughty smile spreading across her face. "Is that what the kids are calling it nowadays?"

"You know, you're sicker than you look," I tell her.

Glory laughs. "So, is that it? No steamy details about your intimate afternoon work session with Mr. Saucy Pants?"

"I'm afraid it was all business," I confess. "Bill and I like to save the steamy stuff for our e-mails."

We pass by a group of twentysomethings having drinks around a bonfire in their backyard. One of the women is laughing ridiculously loudly.

"Hee-hee-hee," Sammie mimics under her breath. "Drunk bitch."

This sends Glory into a fit of hysterics. The girl really is easily amused. Which means I probably shouldn't be too flattered when she splits her ass chuckling at the corny jokes I tell.

"Ya like that, Glory?" I ask.

She shakes her head. "I was just remembering the time Sammie, Grace, and I went camping with my parents."

Oh.

"Oh yeah," Sammie says nostalgically. "And Grace complained the whole time."

"What else is new?" I ask. But my two amigos are too busy strolling down memory lane to bother with my rhetorical questions.

"Remember that walk we took after everyone else fell asleep—when we caught that middle-aged couple doing it?" Glory asks.

"Uh, they were *more* than doing it," Sammie reminds her. "They were busy shooting their own porno."

"Wait, *what* happened?" I ask.

"Yeah, but instead of a couple of big grizzlies walking by," Glory says, once again ignoring my inquiry, "they got two bumbling adolescent extras, laughing their butts off in the background."

"That's too funny," I say to no one in particular. But to be honest, I really don't mind being excluded while Glory and Sammie recapture their middle-school magic. I can always use the time to reflect on my brainy little love magnet as I gaze upon the winter stars.

"Oh, lord," Glory groans, "look at her face. Gee, Sammie, I wonder who she's thinking about."

I'm not sure how long I've been reflecting, but Reminiscence Road has apparently reached its dead end. And it's time for all three of us to leave the memories and dreams behind and snap back into our cold reality.

"Oh my God, that reminds me of Mr. Lenfest!" Sammie exclaims. "Remember what an enormous crush we had on him in seventh grade?"

Or maybe not. Oh well. At least I have visions of Mr. Saucy Pants to keep me warm. Or steaming hot, as the case may be. I can't wait to get home and check my e-mail. I could go for a little extra hot sauce tonight.

# fourteen love letters

Hey there,

How are things going for my favorite city girl? I just finished creating next week's lesson plan for one of my tenth-grade classes, and let's just say if I never hear the words "great" or "expectations" again, it will be too soon. Pathetic, isn't it? Not even 30 years old, and I'm already passing out before nine. If you get this before you go to sleep, try to write me back, okay? I always love waking up to the sight of your name in my inbox. (God, isn't modern courtship romantic? Our

old pal Willy Shakespeare's probably up there somewhere blogging his brains out on the subject, waging a
*new* "Lover's Complaint" on the death of hearts and
flowers . . . *sigh* . . .)

I hope you had fun at your cocktail party.

Thinking of you always (but not in a creepy, stalker
way . . . unless, of course, you'd like me to),
Bill

For shit's sake, how freakin' adorable is he? Adorable,
romantic, witty, sarcastic. If the man were any closer to
perfect, he'd be God. Now, on with the show . . .

**From:** Fiji Pearl <fiji1983@hotmail.com>
**Date:** Wednesday, March 12, 2008 10:34 PM
**To:** Bill Fenowitz <bfenowitz@beaubridgehs.com>
**Subject: Re:** Is it Friday yet?

What's shaking, old man? (j/k) The cocktail party was
lame—a bunch of corporate hotshots engaged in some
kind of bizarre brown-nosing contest—so my friends
and I decided to bail early. We're meeting up for drinks
in about an hour with some interns who weren't invited to sip cosmos with we fancy folk while all those
stuffed suits sniffed butt. Ha ha. But I'm glad I had the

chance to check my e-mail before heading out again. I love coming home/going to sleep/waking up to the sight of your name in my inbox, too. :-)

By the way, that novel you mentioned? Just happens to be the best book I was ever forced to read in high school! I've been trying to get back into the classics. Do you think you could e-mail me your lesson plan to use as a guide or something?

Thinking of you more,
Fiji (like the islands)

P.S. Do they even have blogs in heaven?

**From:** Bill Fenowitz <bfenowitz@beaubridgehs.com>
**Date:** Thursday, March 13, 2008 6:05 PM
**To:** Fiji Pearl <fiji1983@hotmail.com>
**Subject:** Blogging in heaven
**Attachment:** Lesson Plan—GREAT EXPECTATIONS

Fiji,
You really are too funny. I'm sorry last night's shindig was a bust. Cocktail parties usually are. Not that I've ever been to an MTV gala, but there is the school board's annual Christmas party, and believe me, those

things are brutal. I guess we creative types have a harder time with formality than those "stuffed suits" we're supposed to suck up to. Of course, my job probably doesn't sound very creative to an associate producer at MTV like yourself, but take my word, to know a lit-loving wordsmith like me is as close as anyone in these parts gets to artsy.

I'll write more tomorrow. I'm beat from mentoring a couple of students in what was *designed* to be a simple afterschool extra-credit program. Emphasis on the "simple." These two young ladies claim to be best friends, but . . . Who knows, maybe it's a female thing. Did you want to kill your best friend when *you* were fifteen?

Thinking of you,
A very wiped-out Bill

P.S. Enjoy the lesson plan—it's buckets of fun.

Did you hear that? I totally wore him out! He can't stop thinking about me—not Fiji, but *me*. ME! And Grace, too, unfortunately. What is it with her? That slut isn't even here and she's *still* interfering in my relationships. Grace Checkov seriously needs to be put to sleep.

**From:** Fiji Pearl <fiji1983@hotmail.com>
**Sent:** Thursday, March 13, 2008 7:06 PM
**To:** Bill Fenowitz <bfenowitz@beaubridgehs.com>
**Subject: Re:** Blogging in heaven

To my dearest Wiped-Out Willy,
First of all, *you're* the funny one. Secondly, *of course* I wanted to kill my best friend when I was fifteen—I still do! (j/k) Give these girls a break. They're probably just going through some "stuff"—you know, teenage stuff. What are they like, anyway? You never tell me about your students.

Thinking of you more,
Fiji (like the islands)

**From:** Bill Fenowitz <bfenowitz@beaubridgehs.com>
**Sent:** Friday, March 14, 2008 5:31 PM
**To:** Fiji Pearl <fiji1983@hotmail.com>
**Subject:** Curiosity killed the cat

Do you really want to know what my students are like? Because I've gotta warn you: It's not the same as when we were in high school. That's why I usually keep my war stories to myself. But if you're really ready to travel where none of my lady companions have gone before, I'll take you there, beginning with the frightening fact that one of those girls I was telling you about tried to flash me the other day. It was pretty embarrassing, really. I mean, perhaps a guy her own age would've been enthused, but I found it rather sad. She clearly suffers from some kind of self-esteem problem and feels the need to overcompensate by acting out. Her "friend," on the other hand, is a pretty neat kid—listens to classic rock, has an old soul, kind of a quirky sense of humor. Come to think of it, she may just be the only tenth-grade girl I teach who's actually comfortable in her own skin and isn't always trying to be something she's not. The social caste system at Beaubridge is brutal, particularly for females, and unfortunately, most students would rather bow down to the devil than stand up and be individuals.

And that concludes the social commentary portion of this e-mail. Now over to Bob for sports . . . ☺

Shit, seeing myself described through his eyes—I really *am* a pretty neat kid! (Although I prefer the term "sex goddess.") I had no idea Bill had put me on such a pedestal. Not that I completely deserve it. I mean, that part about never trying to be something I'm not . . . If that's really true, then what the piss am I doing now?

**From:** Fiji Pearl <fiji1983@hotmail.com>
**Date:** Friday, March 14, 2008 7:13 PM
**To:** Bill Fenowitz <bfenowitz@beaubridgehs.com>
**Subject: Re:** Curiosity killed the cat

To my favorite news commentator,
That's pretty pathetic about "flasher girl." But I am curious to know more about the other one. I like hearing about your students, and not in some kinky, child molester way. :-) I just like knowing about your work, that's all.

Curious as that dead old cat,
Fiji (like the islands)

**From:** Bill Fenowitz <bfenowitz@beaubridgehs.com>
**Date:** Friday, March 14, 2008 9:21 PM
**To:** Fiji Pearl <fiji1983@hotmail.com>
**Subject:** Here, kitty kitty . . .

Well, I must admit I'm flattered. I wouldn't have thought "Confessions of a High School English Teacher" would be your cup of tea (or should I say your perfect cosmo?). I mean, *you're* the one with the exciting life, but if you really want to know . . .

Her name is CG and her family moved here from Philadelphia a couple of months ago. She's kind of a tomboy, but anyone with eyes can see she's on the cusp of blossoming into a drop-dead knockout, which is probably why "flasher girl" feels so competitive with her . . . Sounds just like *Gossip Girl,* doesn't it? ☺

Missing you even though we've never met,
Bill

A "drop–dead knockout"? Oh my God, could he *be* any more in love with me?

**From:** Fiji Pearl <fiji1983@hotmail.com>
**Date:** Saturday, March 15, 2008 1:07 AM
**To:** Bill Fenowitz <bfenowitz@beaubridgehs.com>
**Subject: Re:** Here, kitty kitty . . .

A drop-dead knockout, huh? Should I be jealous of this CG person? I mean, I know you'd never cross that student-teacher line, but she's not gonna be your student *forever,* Bill . . . How many weeks 'til summer vacation again?

Missing you more,
Fiji (like the islands)

Clever, huh? I've gotta tell you, sometimes I even amaze myself.

**From:** Bill Fenowitz <bfenowitz@beaubridgehs.com>
**Date:** Saturday, March 15, 2008 2:41 PM
**To:** Fiji Pearl <fiji1983@hotmail.com>
**Subject:** 13 weeks, 2 days . . . and counting

My, my, my! What a dirty little mind you have! You're right, though: In a few months, CG won't be my student anymore. But she'll still be *a* student. And even if all laws, moral codes, *and* societal stigmas were magically lifted and I were suddenly free to date every gorgeous girl in this burg, what makes you think I'd start with the teenyboppers? Especially when I could be basking in the tropical warmth of Fiji?

Hot for you,
Bill

P.S. I don't know why this didn't occur to me sooner, but how would you feel about (drumroll, please) finally meeting in person? School's going to be closed for Easter and I thought maybe I could come see you during my time off? That is, unless you have family obligations. Or better plans. Or both. In which case, I'll just go bury my head in the sand and wait to die of shame.

*Fuuuuuuuck!* A real, live, actual meeting? What the elephant's nut am I supposed to do now?

**From:** Fiji Pearl <fiji1983@hotmail.com>
**Date:** Saturday, March 15, 2008 5:53 PM
**To:** Bill Fenowitz <bfenowitz@beaubridgehs.com>
**Subject: Re:** 13 weeks, 2 days . . . and counting

So, you're hot for me now, huh? Talking about this "teenybopper" got you all kinds of in the mood, is that it? I wouldn't feel too bad, Billy Boy. I mean, May–December romances *are* the biggest trend in Hollywood. You and your tomboy could actually make "TomKat" seem like a normal couple. (Imagine that.) And just think, there's only a four-year age difference between you and me. When you're 40, I'll already be 36—not too much variety there. CG, on the other hand, will be just 26—perfect arm candy to accessorize your midlife crisis! All I'm saying is, think about it. One day, this kid could make you look like the biggest stud in Beaubridge (not that you aren't already).

Signed,
Hot and Bothered in Manhattan (aka Fiji, like the islands)

P.S. I'm still not sure what my plans are for Easter. I hail from this fanatically religious Christian family that even goes running to church on *Flag Day,* so, needless to say, my mom would be pretty crushed if I never made it home to LA to celebrate the big resurrection. Still . . . your offer sounds tempting. Why don't you give me your number? That way, even if I don't make up my mind 'til the last minute, I'll still be able to hunt you down ;-)

Good save? Shit, I hope so . . .

# fifteen raising the stakes

"I'm thinking we need to up the ante a little," Grace says, twirling one of her shiny auburn ringlets around her finger. "You know, raise the stakes?"

It's nearly eleven o'clock on Thursday, the first night of Easter break (or spring break, as the school board likes to call it so that we Jewish kids can't claim discrimination come Passover), and we're all sitting cross-legged on Alona's creamy pink satin bedspread. Grace has just suggested a round of Truth and Dare or Torture. Or TDT as it's recently been tagged in the interest of saving syllables. (Alona's brilliant idea, of course. She really is the queen of causes.)

"What do you mean, raise the stakes?" the queen herself asks as she reaches into the Versace china bowl at the center of our circle to grab a nibble of popcorn.

"Well, the last time we played, CG was the only one who actually had a real dare," Grace explains, "and nobody even got tortured."

I lean forward, propping my chin up on my fist. "Do *you* want to be tortured?" *Because that could easily be arranged.* Hand to God, I've been *trying* to love this girl, but what can I say? It's just not happening. I think we reached our boiling point when Bill interrupted yesterday's extra-credit session to rave about how well I've taken to *Great Expectations* and what an asset I've been to class discussion (thank you, Lesson Plan). I literally saw the daggers stabbing through her bonded smile. For Bill's sake—because a little birdie told me he can't stand the vibe between us—I wish I could at least tolerate her in simple doses. But my doctor says I'm allergic to slimy hobags—even a pinch of *skanky bitch* is too much for me to swallow. I mean, do you see how she's totally taken control of my game?

"Nobody *wants* to be tortured," Grace says, scowling at me. "I was just pointing out that things were a little bit tame the first time around. I mean, *we* all thought of a great dare for *you*. But when it came to you pitching in on *our* dares, the night essentially ran out of steam." She glances around the circle, searching for corroboration, but Alona and Sammie manage to avert her gaze. Shows whose side they're on, don't ya think? "I mean, *reaaaally,*" Grace continues loudly, clearly overcompensating for the fact that no one is backing her up on this, "I was practically falling asleep during *my* dare. Like, who *hasn't* been 'challenged' to chug a glass of toilet water before?"

"Um, I haven't," Sammie volunteers.

"Well, you don't count," Grace snaps, turning to glare at her. "And what is with that getup tonight, anyway?" she asks, indicating the bold new Sammie's sudden switch from nightie couture to a more sensible pair of navy sweats. "You look like . . . like . . ." We all watch as she struggles to find the perfect insult. "Like *her!*" she finally concludes, waving her arms at me.

Well, what do you know? I've actually snagged a recruit, managed to level the playing field between normal and "MILF in training."

"It's called 'rebel chic,'" Sammie says, flashing me a smile. "And everyone's doing it."

"Really?" Alona asks incredulously, her blue eyes shimmering at the thought of an undiscovered fashion trend. "I hadn't heard." She sighs, deflating a little. "And I've already bought so many clothes for spring—what a bummer. I'm usually really in tune to these things."

"Don't be too hard on yourself, Lonnie," Grace says, sympathetically patting the Fair One's shoulder. "It doesn't sound so all the rage to *me*. Now," she continues, her eyes shifting coldly between Sammie and me, "can we get back to TDT before it's time to graduate?"

\* \* \*

One down, three to go. Alona has just finished her Truth and Dare set, which included some revealing questions about the status of her virginity (an enigma that remains intact, if only by the worn-out threads on last year's "must-have" G-string), followed by a forty-second, window-front striptease for her dweeby, thirteen-year-old, peeping Tom neighbor. Now it's Sammie's turn.

Knowing that Truth is barely half the fun, Alona and I speed through the cross-examination round, sticking to routine human-sexuality favorites such as "How far have you gotten?" and "Who is your secret celebrity girl crush?" Answering "second base" and "Scarlett Johansson," Sammie promptly turns to Grace, prepared to complete her simple interrogation. But the mischievous glint in Grace's eye sends a frighteningly clear message: She isn't about to make this easy.

"How much do you actually weigh?"

Like a gunshot reverberating through the still of the night, Grace's inquiry forces a silence amongst the rest of us, a murky veil of caution that no one is willing to penetrate. No one, that is, except for the wicked witch herself.

"Well, Sammie?"

Alona casts a worried glance in my direction. Hell, even *she* knows you don't ask someone like Sammie to talk numbers. I mean, it's one thing to take a girl who clearly suffers from body image disturbances and have someone else kindly remind her she's big, but to ask her how much she *weighs?* Well, that just crosses the line. I told you: Alona really *is* a sweet person. As long as everything's pretty and perfect and you always do exactly what she expects of you.

"You know, we don't have all night," Grace adds, the pressure mounting.

"I realize that," Sammie says.

"Well?" Grace prods. "Don't tell me you don't know. Any girl who says she doesn't know how much she weighs is either lying or a total cow who's just too ashamed to step on a scale. So . . . which are you?"

*"Grace!"* Alona shrieks.

I shake my head. "You bitch."

*"CG!"* Alona is beside herself now, completely dismayed. "Come on, you guys. Can't we all just chill out and be happy?"

"No," Sammie says. Alona turns to stare at her,

stunned. Has old kick-around Sammie taken this rebel thing too far? Is she actually starting to act out against her ruler and revolt? "I mean, yes, I can chill out and be happy," she clarifies. Well, so much for *that*. "But I'm not discussing my weight . . . with any of you." Still, she *has* come a very long way.

"I can definitely respect that," I say. "Let's move on."

"All right," Grace concedes, still focusing on Sammie. "How about I just dare you to hop on the scale, then? This way, you won't have to discuss anything."

"Come on, Grace," Alona says. "Just let it go."

"Besides, you know we all have to agree on the dare," I point out.

"And anyway, you still get to ask her a question," Alona adds, "since she didn't answer your other one."

"I've got a better idea," Sammie says. "How about Grace forfeits her question in exchange for complete authority over my dare?"

"Meaning?" Grace asks, a scheming smile playing upon her creepy little lips.

"Meaning you pick the dare, I do it. As long as it's not weight related."

"Are you sure?" Grace asks. "Because, you know Alona's like the angel on my shoulder, always keeping me in line. And I've noticed that *this* one," she says, nodding toward me, "tends to have your back lately." She grabs a piece of popcorn, rotates it slowly between her thumb and forefinger . . . crushes it. "There's no telling what you're going to get when you roll the dice with just me."

"I'm willing to take my chances," Sammie tells her.

"Don't say I didn't warn you."

★ ★ ★

Okay, that was it—the fourth ring. Maybe she's not home.

"She's not answering," I tell Sammie, who is seated at Alona's desk, cradling her fuzzy, fuchsia *they skinned a Maltese so I could have this* phone. "Hang up."

"No way!" Grace barks in a sort of whisper-yell, her hand covering the mouthpiece of the sleek black cordless she's sharing with Alona. Crouched on the floor next to the vanity like a couple of bandits about to pull off a major heist, the two of them look as if they actually believe Sammie's victim can see us. If that were the case, I'd be wearing a giant bag over my head. One with the word SELLOUT written all over it. Hell, maybe I'd even be lucky enough to suffocate to death before she picked up and said—

"Hello?"

"Um . . ." Sammie clears her throat, trying to disguise her voice. From my position on the bed, holding an older, clunkier cordless from the Speltons' game room, I give her a nod, letting her know that I've still got her back—even if this is the worst thing I've ever seen her do. "Is Glory Finklefuss there?"

"This is Glory." There is a long, gaping pause, and I feel my heart sink about a thousand stories, down through my toes, the sand, and the soil, and into the firepits of hell. "Who's this?" Fortunately for Grace's scheme, Alona has a blocked telephone number; otherwise Caller ID would've forced us up shit's creek without a paddle before we'd even set sail.

"Uh, this is Bernadette Samson," Sammie says, reading from the script Grace created for her.

"Who?"

"I write for the *Beaubridge Beat,* your school paper. You may not have heard of me. I just transferred here from Singapore. My father's in the army." Geez, I hope Grace isn't planning on winning any Pulitzers with this piece of crap.

"Oh . . . Can I ask why you're calling me?"

"Um . . ." Using her index finger, Sammie frantically skims the page in search of her next line. It seems Grace only wrote the scene one way, never stopping to consider that Glory might throw her leading lady a curveball by actually *talking back.* "I'm sorry to call so late,"

Sammie says finally, "but I was assigned a story for the paper on how certain kids feel about the social higher archie at Beaubridge High."

*Higher archie?* Oh no, she didn't. *Oh, Sammie.* Giggles erupt from the other side of the room as Alona and Grace toss their phone onto the bed, collapsing in a convulsive fit of laughter.

"You mean hierarchy," Glory says kindly, correcting her.

"Oh yeah." Sammie shrugs, her face flushing a little. "I thought that's what I said. Well, anyway, can I interview you?"

"Well, sure, but why me?"

Alona and Grace crawl over to the bed to grab their phone, propping their elbows up on the comforter.

"Well . . ." Sammie's stuck again.

I put my hand over my mouthpiece, turning to Grace. "Go help her."

"Are you *kidding?* I can't remember the last time I laughed this hard."

*Whore.*

"Oh!" Sammie seems to have found a satisfying answer to Glory's question. "I'm sorry to call so late, but I was assigned a story for the paper on how certain kids feel about the social *hierarchy* at Beaubridge High.

Oh, wait . . ." She begins rifling through her script. "I mean . . . I just transferred here from Singapore. My father's in the army."

Glory begins to chuckle, that genuine warm-hearted chuckle that told me she'd be a blast to hang out with even before I really knew her. "Didn't you just say that?"

"Yeah," Sammie concedes, discouraged. She looks over at the three of us, watching her from the bed, and mouths *I can't do it*.

"It's okay," Glory tells her. "You can do this. Just don't be so nervous. You're doing *fine*. If I can make one suggestion, though, Bernadette, I wouldn't call anyone else until tomorrow afternoon. I don't know how they did things in Singapore, but in Beaubridge, your best bet for conducting interviews for the school paper would be *before* midnight." She chuckles again, and I think I'm just about ready to leapfrog out the window—straight into the arms of Alona's thirteen-year-old peeping Tom if I have to. Anything to avoid hearing the rest of this. Then again, it's sort of like bearing witness to a cataclysmic car crash. You'd do anything to erase your involvement, but seeing as you're already *there*—and the damage is already done—you may as well just sit back and watch the wreck.

"Okay," Sammie says, shooting me one final glance of desperation before returning to her script. "My first question is, would it be fair to say you're not exactly Miss Popularity?"

"I guess so."

"Would it be even more accurate to call you a nerd?"

"Well . . ."

"What would you say is the number one reason the cool crowd won't give you the time of day?"

"Well, that's not entirely true." *Oh, fuckers. Don't say it.* "CG Silverman and I are . . ." *Don't say* friends. "Well, we're neighbors and—"

"Could it be because of your frizzed-out Ronald McDonald fro?" Sammie interrupts, reeling her back into the script. And not a moment too soon.

"Huh?"

"Or what about those shitty—sorry, *shifty*—bug eyes of yours, always monitoring Grace Checkov and the rest of her posse like some paranoid schizo beetle?" Well, that was a mouthful, and notice that when Grace holds the pen, it's suddenly *her* posse.

"I thought you said we never met," Glory stammers. "Did . . . did someone put you up to this?"

"I just have a few more questions," Sammie says quietly, no doubt feeling like a world-class piece of shit at the thought of all the good times we "haven't" had with Glory over the last five weeks—you know, the afternoon walks we "didn't" take, the middle school bond they "never" recaptured, the inside jokes they "aren't" starting to bust out all over again. "If you were to credit one of the following for influencing your unique fashion sense, who would it be?" Sammie asks. "The Farmer in the Dell, our Amish friends out in Lancaster, or the early nineties rap duo Kriss Kross?"

"I'm sorry . . . *What?*"

"Do you still have irritable bowel syndrome?"

A bone-chilling blast of dead air rushes through the receiver. I swear, it's these long, dreadful silences that always make the most noise. I glance over at Grace—sitting there so smug in her designer nightgown, with her French manicured fingernails and salon-sculpted brows—and wonder what the hell it is she has against the defenseless "schizo beetle" we've been tormenting with this retarded prank. I mean, any rivalry they may have had back in the day has clearly resulted in a victory for Grace. By high school standards—by Beaubridge standards—she's leading the race by a landslide. *So, why do you hate her so much?* I want to ask. *What does Glory Finklefuss have on you?*

"Um, how would you know about that?" Glory says finally. "I only ever told two people, and that was years ago."

"Uh . . ." Sammie throws us all a panicked shrug. *Gee, I wonder who the two people were.* "I think I heard someone mention it," she fumbles, accidentally dropping Bernadette's sugary falsetto.

"Samara?"

Holy bowel movement, this is bad. *She's onto you, Sammie. Think fast.*

"No, it's, um, Bernadette Samson," she says, clearing her throat. "From the *Beaubridge Beat*. You may not have heard of me. I just transferred here from Singapore."

"Save it, Samara. I recognize your voice. Let me guess. Grace put you up to this and you just *couldn't* say no? Well, here's a quote for your newspaper article: Grace Checkov is a self-serving, vindictive, egomaniacal bitch, and what goes around comes around, so she'd better watch her back...You got that, Gracie?"

CLICK.

Okaaaay...now what? Glory's unexpected verbal assault has left all of us visibly numb. Nobody's moving, and nobody's laughing—least of all Grace, who looks like she just sat on a chainsaw. Is that anger I see erupting under her perfect porcelain pores ... or could it actually be fear?

Sammie hangs up Alona's fuzzy, pink phone and stares down at the floor, clutching her stomach. I feel sick, too. Like maybe if I got up and ralphed all over Grace's smug little face, I'd feel better. Maybe I should try it. Just to see.

Alona follows Sammie's lead. Shutting off the cord-less she was sharing with Grace, she sets it down on her bed—slowly and carefully—as if it were a loaded revolver. I'm the last one to hang up, probably because letting go of the phone means our little prank on Glory is really over. And now it's time to face what we've done.

"Somebody please say something," Alona pipes up. "It's getting creepy in here. And tonight was supposed to be fun."

Grace shakes her head. "That girl is lucky I don't leave right now and go slit her throat while she's sleep-ing." Assessing the disturbed looks on our faces as we all digest this newer, and even uglier, side of Grace—or should I say, Grace the Ripper—she goes on to say, "Oh, come on. Did you hear how that reject *talked* to me? Calling *me* a vindictive, egomaniacal bitch?"

"Yeah," Sammie scoffs. "Clearly, she doesn't know you at all."

In spite of my queasiness, I can't help but smile at her artfully aimed jab.

"Ooh, check out the attitude on this one," Grace purrs, her eyes lighting up. "Do you have a problem with me, Sammie? Or is this newfound sarcasm all just part of your rebel makeover?"

"Why'd you do that to me?" Sammie asks.

"Do what to you?" Grace says in an exaggeratedly slow

and raspy tone, clearly poking fun at Sammie's voice. "You'll have to excuse me. I don't speak cavewoman."

"You know what I'm referring to," Sammie insists. "You sold me down the river with Glory. You set me up. You knew she'd realize it was me after I mentioned her stomach condition."

"How would I have known that?" Grace asks, acting bored as she casually strolls over to Alona's desk, where she logs on to MySpace and begins surfing user profiles. "Maybe I thought the little freak was proud of her intestinal turmoil. How was I supposed to know she'd only told just you and me? It's not like we were *that* close."

"We were *best friends,*" Sammie counters. And I've gotta say, Grace's reaction is damn near priceless. Of course, all the self-serving egomaniac really cares about is *Alona's* reaction, which she has just whipped her head over her shoulder in a complete 180 to gauge. But our beautiful shepherd betrays no response. She's too busy falling asleep.

"We were *not,*" Grace snaps, turning her attention back to Sammie. "And why do you care so much, anyway, *Samara?* Is some random middle-school acquaintance really all that important to you? What, do you still hang out with her every day behind our backs or something?"

"Yeah," Sammie snorts. "We're having an affair. You can read all about it in *Us Weekly.* And for your information," she continues, "I've always preferred 'Samara.' It was you who christened me 'Sammie' once we got to high school because it was *oh sooo important* I change my image."

"I never knew that," Alona says, snapping out of her stupor.

"Me neither," I add.

"Yeah, well . . ." Sammie looks down at the floor. "There are a lot of things you guys don't know about me."

Alona yawns. *Yawns?* In the middle of a cliffhanger like that? "All this tension is making me tired. Can we call, like, a recess or something and reconvene tomorrow night for Grace and CG's dares?"

"I think that would be a good idea," Grace agrees, turning to shoot some more death rays at Sammie. "We could *all* use our beauty sleep."

Christ almighty, have you ever met such a *bitch?* Me neither. All I know for sure is that one day, sooner than later, that bitch is gonna pay.

\* \* \*

Friday, March 21, 2008
Confessions of a Teenage Call Girl
Greetings, MySpacers! And welcome to my

first blog. It's late at night—or early in the morning, depending upon which side of the sky you're looking at—and I never went to bed. Or should I say "sleep," since I did spend the last three hours making the feathers fly out of a certain lucky someone's cozy down mattress. We just didn't have resting on the brain.

A lot of you know me as that sassy bitch from Beaubridge who hangs with Alona S. You come on here thinking that adding me as a friend will be your secret key inside my world. You think because I click "approve" to your piddling little friend invites, it actually means I know who you are. I'm here to tell you: I don't.

As for those of you out there who don't go to Beaubridge—my dozens of "friends" who only wanted to add me because I'm so smoking hot—I've got a message for you, too.

I've got a message for all of you . . .

Beauty is only skin deep. And you should be glad you don't know the real me—a girl who trades sex for money, money for drugs, drugs to dull the pain of what she's become. That is the world I've excluded you from. The world of Grace Checkov, a worthless, dope-addicted high school hooker.

By the way, if I happen to sound like one of those "This is your brain on drugs" PSAs from a VH-1 *I Love the 80s* special, it's only because this *is* my brain on drugs. Why else would I be sitting here at 3:45 a.m. spilling my soul to you losers?

Anyway, as my mother used to say, "It's time to say good night, Gracie." So . . . good night.

# sixteen  easy, breezy, beautiful cover boy

**JAS88:** Guess who's home?
**JJ_Pearl:** Hey, stranger! When did you get in?
**JAS88:** About a half hour ago. I haven't even un-packed yet. After the family finished fussing over me, I came directly upstairs to see if you were online.
**JJ_Pearl:** And here I am.

It would be a lie if I said I hadn't been looking for-ward to this moment all day. Despite what happened at Alona's last night—despite the nauseated, dreadful feel-ing in the pit of my stomach as I fell asleep thinking about Glory—I still woke up with a tingle in my nether regions. Tonight's the night Jordan and I have been talk-ing about for weeks. Our big clandestine reunion—the long-awaited encore to our first and only hookup, the climax of our ongoing online flirtation. My lips quiver every time I think about kissing him again.

> **JAS88:** You still sleeping over tonight?
> **JJ_Pearl:** That's the plan.
> **JAS88:** It'll be good to see you again.
> **JJ_Pearl:** Yeah, I've heard I'm pretty easy on the eyes.
> **JAS88:** LOL . . So, how've you been?
> **JJ_Pearl:** You mean since we last chatted two days ago?
> **JAS88:** It seems like years to me.
> **JJ_Pearl:** You're such a bullshitter. You'll say just about anything to get a gal to spend the night.
> **JAS88:** Maybe . . . but that doesn't mean I'm not interested in how you are. How was your little pajama party with the bimbo squad last night?
> **JJ_Pearl:** Good. Tons of fun, as usual.

Oh, come on. Like I'm gonna tell him what really happened. How I managed to stab one of my best friends in the back just for the sake of fitting in. How I've been aching to call her all day but just couldn't work up the balls to pick up the phone. I mean, what would I even say to Glory now? Every time I think of her, all I can picture is her wounded voice on the other end of the line last night when she discovered Sammie's betrayal. I don't know what I'd do if she were to ever find out that I betrayed her, too.

> **JAS88:** I bet tonight will be even more fun. Once the real party begins, I mean.
> **JJ_Pearl:** Oh yeah? You sound pretty sure of yourself.
> **JAS88:** I have to be. Do you think I could've gotten this far in life on good looks alone?
> **JJ_Pearl:** Confident *and* modest. You really are a catch, Jordan.
> **JAS88:** Ah, so you noticed.
> **JJ_Pearl:** Hey, I'm a quick study. You think I could've gotten this far on *my* good looks alone?
> **JAS88:** Touché.

Chatting with Jordan has gotten so easy, so breezy. So beautiful Cover Girl. Sometimes it's like we're in our own little bubble and nothing else matters but sexy innuendos and who can think of the best comeback line. If only life were as simple as my IM sessions with Jordan, I'd never have to worry about what a dick I've become. The whole Glory crank-call situation could just melt away into yesterday and I'd never have to think about it again. Talk about getting off easy. And speaking of getting off . . .

**JJ_Pearl:** So, tell me more about this private party you have planned for tonight.

**JAS88:** Let's just say both guests will come happy and leave happier.

**JJ_Pearl:** Hey, I just remembered another one of your good qualities.

**JAS88:** Do tell.

**JJ_Pearl:** You're so subtle.

**JAS88:** Subtlety is overrated, my dear. Now let's start planning your escape . . .

# seventeen the ultimate dare

By refusing to budge on the weight issue last night, Sammie seems to have set a new precedent for TDT: skipping over the first T, that being the truth, in the interest of going straight to the heart of the game.

"After all," Alona pointed out when we reconvened earlier this evening, "the real risk lies in the dare. And Grace *did* say we should raise the stakes."

If it were up to me, I'd have dared Grace to jump off the Empire State Building without a parachute, but Alona had already thought of "a good one" that probably didn't involve mutilation or death. "Providing CG and Sammie approve it, of course," she said, batting her long, honey-colored lashes in a way that beseeched us to agree before we'd even heard it. Then again, maybe it was a good thing for Alona to be in charge of Grace's dare. I'm way too young to go to jail for murder. "I want Grace to act out a porno with Iggy." Iggy is Grace's long-suffering teddy bear. This was going to be interesting . . .

Oh yeah, I forgot. Nothing Grace does is worth watching—not even when she's gyrating in her bra and panties aboard some poor, unsuspecting stuffed animal that would probably bite her in the crotch and give her rabies if given the chance to come to life. Though I am grateful to see her in such a free-spirited mood. Sounds oxymoronic, I know, but Grace's good spirits tell me she hasn't logged on to her MySpace account all day, which means the vindictive little bitch is still in for the shock of her life when she discovers the oh-so-brilliant blog I posted in her name. Oh, come on, *somebody* had to get her back for what she did to Sammie and Glory with that evil crank call. Lucky for me, she accidentally left the screen open on her homepage last night. How could I *not* take advantage of that? She practically made me do it.

When Grace has finished molesting her favorite childhood toy, the focus turns to me.

"We have the ultimate dare for you, CG," Alona says after a brief huddle with the others.

"The ultimate dare?" I ask, my heart thumping. I'm not gonna like this, am I? "Can't wait to hear it."

"We want you to call Mr. Fenowitz," Alona says, her eyes widening with excitement. *Okaaaay. CG, meet the Ultimate Dare. Ultimate Dare, meet CG.* "And set up a date for him and Fiji to meet at the Larmont Hotel to-morrow night."

"Oh, come on," I say, laughing her off. I mean, I fig-ured she was serious about the phone call (*Note to self: Next time the hottest teacher at Beaubridge gives you his digits, go ahead and eighty-six the public service announcement*), but she can't possibly think I could keep the Fiji thing going in person. How *do* you set up a date to meet someone who isn't allowed to look at you?

"You're going to tell him it's a masquerade ball," Alona continues. "Well, a miniball, anyway." She glances around the circle, grinning from ear to ear. "Just you and a few close friends."

"We'll all be wearing masks and so will he," Grace says.

Sammie gives me an encouraging nod. "They do it all the time in those cheesy Hilary Duff–type movies, and no one ever knows who anyone is."

"But that's Hollywood," I point out, "and I'm no Hil-ary Duff." Well, at least God did me *one* favor. "What if he tries to lift my mask?" Wait, *what* mask? The only mask I own goes with the Freddy Krueger costume I lent to my "ex-boyfriend" Alex last Halloween. Not ex-actly my idea of a great first-date impression.

"He won't," Alona assures me. "Lifting other people's masks goes against masquerade etiquette."

Grace hands over the phone. "Now dial."

For shit's sake, I only asked for Bill's number to see if he'd give it to me, to maybe call and hang up once in a while just to bask in the sound of his frustrated hellos. I never actually planned on a *legitimate* conversation, let alone having one in front of a live studio audience who'd be listening in on their respective receivers. And look at Grace—just sitting there with that sly little grin on her face, waiting for me to fail and make a life-sized asshole out of myself. God knows she was the mastermind behind this sticky shenanigan. I mean let's face it, Alona's just not that clever. Or that evil. This is gonna be a freakin' disaster.

"Oh, and don't forget to tell him," Grace says, covering her mouthpiece as the phone begins its timorous, terrified ring, "that the theme of the ball is lingerie. Think Hugh Hefner and the Playboy Mansion." *What?* "We're all going in our underwear."

# eighteen kissing frogs

Jordan said he'd leave the light on for me, that I should wait until the others fall asleep, then make a break for it. I've gotta tell you, I'm not nearly as nervous as I was last time. Maybe because we're old IM buddies now, and this isn't some stupid dare and I'm not wearing one of his sister's silly frilly slipamadrips. If anything, I'm excited. Okay, make that horny as hell. Not that I plan to leave his room tonight with my virginity dangling by the thread of my G-string, but I'm certainly planning to check my goody two-shoes at the door. I mean, what kind of self-respecting rebel is a big bucket of wholesome when the lights go out, anyway? Besides, we've been building up to this booty call for *weeks*. I'm sure Jordan's expecting his share of fireworks. God knows *I* am. I just wish I could shake the feeling that I'm cheating on Bill.

With bated breath, I twist the knob on Alona's bedroom door, quietly closing it behind me. Cautiously placing one foot in front of the other, I begin to creep down the spacious shadow-filled hallway as if walking a narrow tightrope. See, *this* is the part that freaks me out—the idea of getting caught.

You know what else is pretty freaky? Having a hand thrown over your mouth in the middle of the night while your body is yanked into some cold, merciless chamber of death... otherwise known as the john. Okay, so my imagination got the best of me. I take a second to catch my breath as Jordan, standing there in nothing but his shower-moist skin and a towel, stares down into my bewildered eyes, smiling. *Oy vey.*

"You scared me," I whisper. "I was on my way to your room. I didn't even hear the shower running."

"I was hoping to surprise you," he whispers back. Without breaking his gaze, he glides a finger down his perfectly cut, made-for-TV abs, touching a warm droplet of water to my lips. And we kiss. *Oh, God.* What was I saying before about Bill?

Jordan lifts me onto the sink. And I immediately fall in. (Sexy, huh?) But he isn't the least bit fazed. Nothing can break his stride as he scoops me up with his strong, powerful hands, pulling me so close I can barely breathe (not that I'm *at all* complaining). I could never imagine doing this with Bill. I want to *marry* Bill. I want to put the rest of my youth on fast forward just so that he can finally see me as more than jailbait. I want to go to museums and restaurants and movies with him and lie in bed every night cuddling in his arms while he reads me saucy passages from Shakespeare and Dickens. But this . . .

Jordan's fingers have begun to wander up my shirt. "I want you so bad," he moans.

*This* I can only imagine doing with Jordan. I guess now I understand why married women have affairs with their gardeners.

★ ★ ★

Don't ask how it happened. It's like I blinked and there we were. Well, first his towel "fell" on the floor. And *then* I blinked. I don't know . . . It all went by so fast. Not *it*-it—don't get the wrong idea; we didn't go all the way—but lying on a towel with a naked college man was more than I bargained for when I decided to ditch the prude 'tude.

It's not that I feel bad or anything. I mean, I kept *my* pants on the whole time. Besides, my virginity's still more intact than Alona's. And even if it weren't, there are tons of girls my age who have already done it. I just want my first time to be special, not a stolen moment on a bathroom floor with some guy I can't tell anyone about. Still, they say you have to kiss a lot of frogs before you find your prince, and if Bill and I can't be together for another two years and change, I couldn't think of a more appealing frog to bide my adolescence with.

So, then, what the hell is bothering me?

Back in Alona's room again, staring up into the pitch-black nothingness, I reach under the covers of my sleeping bag, feeling for the old woven fabric bracelet I wear on my right wrist.

"It looks like you never take this thing off," Jordan said tonight as we lay there making the tiles sweat on the bathroom floor. "Who gave it to you?"

I wasn't about to tell him it was a middle-school graduation gift from Alex, a "best friend" I haven't talked to in months, a guy his sister thinks is my emotionally unstable ex, a person who *would* be my boyfriend if I hadn't been in such a rush to chuck the old CG and become somebody special.

"Nobody," I said, putting my arm around him so the bracelet was no longer in view. "Nobody gave it to me. I just have it."

"Oh yeah?" he asked, playfully tweaking my chin. "Kind of like you just have this mouth?" He leaned down, bit my lower lip. "Or this nose? Or these . . ." Well, you get the idea.

So, *that's* what's been nagging at me, detracting from the moist, gooey posthookup flutter I should be feeling? The fact that Alex Kerper is on my mind? Or is it the fact that he never really left?

Don't get me wrong. I'm not in love with him or anything. Not anymore. We don't even *know* each other anymore. And I'm still glad I said no when he asked me to go with him. Can you imagine how that—my having a boyfriend back home—would've spoiled things with Jordan? Not to mention my future plans with Bill. Let alone *Fiji's* present plans with Bill, which reminds me: I really should get my beauty rest. The girls and I have a date with Frederick's of Hollywood at noon.

# nineteen barely legal

So, here we are. The penthouse suite at the Larmont Hotel, located in exotic Larmont, Pennsylvania, two suburbs north of Beaubridge. My watch says 8:47, which means Bill should be here in thirteen minutes. I don't even want to know how many laws we've broken so far.

"Exactly *how* are you going to explain this charge on your father's bill?" I ask Alona, whose pink satin-and-lace teddy and strappy silver heels make her look like she's just crawled out of a steamy *Maxim* spread, which means that out of the four of us, she's the only one who can even remotely pass for twentysomething. "I mean, I know it's your card, but he still writes the checks, doesn't he?"

"Of course he does. But . . ." She smiles innocently, stretching out on the living room's white leather sofa while I pace back and forth by the entertainment center. "*Somebody* has a big birthday coming up. I'll just tell him we threw you a party." Is she out of her mind?

"A thirty-five-hundred-dollar party?"

Alona shrugs. "He probably won't even check the statement."

"You mean he won't notice the fact that his little girl has been doing time at the Larmont Hotel?"

She holds her hands out in front of her as if to say she's as lost for answers as I am.

"You've got to come up with a better lie," I tell her.

"CG," Grace butts in. "Just let it go. Mr. Spelton is *not* going to find out."

"Well, accidents do happen," I tell her. "Not that I'm worried." I mean, hey, rebels don't worry about anything, remember? "It's just that my birthday isn't for another three weeks," I explain, turning back to Alona, "and our fathers work together—he's gonna know you're not telling the truth."

She sighs heavily, exasperated, and I think it's the first time I've ever seen the light go out of her sparkling blue eyes. "My father doesn't know anything, CG. He doesn't care what I do—half the time, he's not even around to notice. *I'm* the one who told *him* your dad works for Klytech."

"Huh?"

"It was after my mother told *me*. She saw your dad's file on his desk and thought I might be interested in getting to know the new girl who was moving to Beaubridge."

"And were you?" I ask, not sure if I actually want to hear the answer.

"She was interested in getting to know her father," Grace says, taking a seat beside her friend on the sofa. She puts her arms around Alona, and next to one another, with Grace in a red teddy and gold strappy heels, they look something like the Doublemint Twins. Only Grace's "double mints" required much more pushing and padding in order to make her pass for postpubescent. Then again, so did mine. I just hope my miracle boob job isn't quite *that* obvious. "You don't know how things are in other people's families," Grace continues. "Not everyone can live like the Waltons."

It's a cliché, I know—even the pretty ones have problems. But if I'm aware of this universal truth, how come I never thought it would apply to Alona Spelton? I guess I've just been so caught up in making sure she knows *me*—the me I've wanted her to know, anyway—that I forgot one of the first rules of friendship: It works both ways.

"I'm sorry," I tell her. "It must suck not having a relationship with your dad." I honestly wouldn't know. My father's in my face every minute of every day. He yells just to show he cares. But considering the alternative . . . Well, at least I'm not destined to end up some shopaholic exhibitionist with Daddy issues. Still, while I always figured the Klytech connection was the main reason for my swift acceptance into the inner circle, I didn't think it was the *only* reason.

"Wait, don't get the wrong idea," Alona says suddenly. "I wasn't using you. I mean, I guess I *sort of* was, but only in the beginning." She smiles. "Before I fell in love with your crazy rebel spirit."

"And when was that?" I ask, trying not to sound as curious—or desperate—as I really feel.

She thinks for a second. "Probably right around the time of our first sleepover, when you introduced us all to TDT." *Uh, you mean when I totally lied my ass off about my scandalous sex-filled past and started earning my stripes as group daredevil?* "Don't be mad," she says. "It's not like Grace or Sammie were in on it or anything."

"I just know Lonnie so well," Grace gloats, her demonic eyes beaming with possession. "I was able to put two and two together."

"About what?" asks Sammie as she emerges from the

bathroom, where she insisted on changing in private. "And what wasn't I in on?"

"Never mind," Grace says, her face contorting as she assesses Sammie's party gear—an ankle-length, blue chiffon nightgown with a matching long-sleeved robe (or is that a shower curtain?). It totally looks like something Bea Arthur would've worn on *The Golden Girls*. And P.S., I think the robe has shoulder pads. It's obvious this whole lingerie theme has made my body-conscious pal a bit squeamish. Not that I haven't done my fair share of squirming, too. It's the reason I went with the black innerwear/outerwear corset, matching pair of boy shorts, and thigh high "dominatrix boots"—so I could *look* slutty without actually having to show anything.

God, I wonder what Alex would say if he could see me like this. I still remember the time we stumbled upon his dad's secret stash of nudie magazines and literally pissed ourselves laughing—those models were all such freakin' bimbo cheeseballs. Alex didn't get how any guy could be turned on by such obvious implants and ridiculously staged *do me* faces. He never cared for that sort of manufactured sex appeal—you know, the Pamela Anderson kind. Then again, Alex was definitely not your typical guy. Maybe that's why our friendship worked so well—because I definitely wasn't your typical girl either. That is, until I became part of the Four Tops and started dressing like a runaway hooker.

"By the way, CG, if I haven't said so already," Grace continues, turning away from Sammie, "I really like what you're wearing tonight. And I think Bill's going to also."

I feel my jaw drop and bounce back up off my organically enhanced bosom—why in fuck's kingdom is she being so nice to me? "Are you *drunk?*"

Grace laughs. "No, but I will be soon." She looks at Alona. "You've got the vodka, right?"

Okay, pause it. Remember that thing I mentioned earlier about breaking the law? Well, here's the scoop. We needed someone eighteen or older to sign for this suite—hotel policy or something—so Jordan and Alona came at around six o'clock, pretending to be a couple. (I know, *ew*, incest, but, hey, you've gotta do what you've gotta do, right?) Thinking he was helping his sister arrange for "some lame high school party," Jordan filled out the paperwork and signed for the room while Alona paid with her charge. The two of them then went to buy alcohol using the fake ID some college senior gave Jordan when he first got to Penn State. (It says his name is Angus Tuckleberg Jr., but that's beside the point.) Alona then dropped Jordan off at home and picked the three of us up, naturally failing to sign us in as additional guests of her and her "husband's." Okay, did you get all that? Me neither.

Still, I guess, technically speaking, *I* haven't broken any laws yet. Rules, maybe. But not laws. Then again, the night is still young . . .

"Vodka, check!" Alona says happily. "I'm just waiting to pour it into the punch." She stands up, smoothing out the crinkles in her teddy. "Everything's in the dining room. Cups, party snacks, napkins in case things get messy." She gives me a naughty look, and I feel as if I've just swallowed a giant jarful of butterflies. If that's the case, I hope they all start a massive pissing battle in my mouth—I don't think my throat's been this parched since that time I got lost in space without my freeze-dried Red Bull. "Oh, and I forgot to mention," she adds on her way into the other room, "my brother said he might come by later. But I told him not to bother showing up without reinforcements."

"Woo-hoo!" Grace cheers. "More alcohol!"

"You mean Jordan's coming *here?*" I yelp.

All of a sudden, there's a knock at the door. I glance down at my watch. 8:59. *Oh, holy mother of vodka.* I think I literally see my pulse.

Alona flitters back into the living room, her face flushed with excitement.

"Put your mask on," Sammie whispers, squeezing my arm. "It's showtime."

★ ★ ★

Two hours and twelve minutes later, Grace is on her umteenth glass of punch; Sammie, her umpteenth plate of food; and Alona's passing out in the corner. As for Bill and Fiji . . . Well, let's just say I've seen better first dates. Which totally doesn't make any sense. I mean, we have such fabulous digital chemistry, and in person, Bill and *CG* totally hit it off every day. But something about in-the-flesh "party Bill" just really isn't much of a party. On a social level, he's . . . I don't know . . . sort of *retarded*. For the last half hour, he's been prattling on about some lame-ass grad school essay as if it were the second coming of the Beatles.

". . . so, I ended up making that my thesis," he, at long last, concludes. And not nearly soon enough. I think my ears are starting to bleed. "Because if you stop to consider the relevance of Chaucer . . ." Oh, *sweet God,* I swear if I had a rope, I'd hang myself. No wonder this man spends all his free time lurking in chat rooms for the "single and looking." For as cute as he is, for as charming and witty as he appears in print, Bill has got to be the *most boring nimrod* I've ever met in my entire life!

And the biggest buffoon, oblivious not only to the rat's ass I could give about Chaucer but also to the severe generation gap between him and his fellow party peeps. I mean, is the man that socially stunted that he can't even sniff out the difference between a fifteen-year-old girl and a woman his own age? Sheesh. Back in the day, Alex and I would've busted a nut making fun of this dork. I'm talking inside jokes out the bumhole. Too bad I'll never get a chance to tell him the story. Oh, well. All I can think about now is saving myself.

"Would you excuse me just one second?" I ask, jumping to my feet. "I need to go powder my nose." Now, *there's* an expression I've never used before.

"Oh, sure, go ahead," he says, unfazed by the interruption. "When you get back, I'll finish telling you all about the parallels between Faulkner and Dickens."

"Oh, goodie!" I exclaim, forcing a polite smile as I make my escape.

Well, isn't this just a peach—somebody's yakking in the john. I can totally hear them heaving and wretching beneath the dull murmur of the running faucet. There's no way I'm going in there now. The only thing worse than hearing yak is smelling yak.

"Nice going, Grace," I mumble. "How many glasses did it take?"

"Not sure. I'll let you know when *I'm* the one hanging my head over that ivory bowl, praying to the porcelain gods." What the . . . ?

I turn around to spot Grace, and yeah, she's tipsy—as evidenced by her lack of balance and the fact that she now has her arms around me (okay, so maybe she's more like *hammered*)—but all her guts remain remarkably intact. Alona's still lying like a cracked-out zombie on the living room floor, so that only leaves . . .

"How much did Sammie have to drink?" I ask.

Grace shrugs carelessly, letting go of me, stumbling a little in her gold stilettos. "I *thought* she was drinking from the sissy bowl all night. You know, deep down," she coos, suddenly descending into baby talk, "our *wittle* Samara's just a good girl like you."

"What makes you say that?"

"She doesn't like to sip the naughty stuff, either," Grace says, putting a covert finger to her lips as if the spiked punch bowl is now our sinful "wittle" secret.

Whoa, stop the presses! I can't have Grace thinking I'm some kind of law-abiding citizen here. CG Silverman is supposed to be the anti-sissy, everybody's favorite bad girl. I know that in the morning, Grace won't even remember whether I sipped the naughty nectar or not. But I still find myself saying . . .

"Are you *kidding?* I love booze."

"You do?" she asks.

"Hell, yeah. You should have seen me last year—I was, like, a borderline alcoholic. I used to black out so often, I couldn't even tell the difference between night and day."

Grace laughs so hard, I think she pops a blood vessel or something. Would it be wrong to say I sort of like her this way, that I actually prefer this sloshed alien species known as Hammerhead Grace? "So, you don't drink at all anymore, then?" she asks. "Were you, like, in rehab or something?"

"Yes!" That's perfect. Rather than saying I find the smell of alcohol more repugnant than the smell of yak and would sooner slam back a pint of warm piss than a bottle of beer, rather than saying even badasses like me worry about getting busted, I just tell her, "I did some serious time at this clinic out west trying to kick my addiction. I've been clean for almost ten months." When did I officially become the world's biggest bullshitter? And why, might I ask, am I so *freakin'* fantastic at it?

"Wow, I had no idea," Grace says regretfully. Then, she hiccups and for some mysterious reason feels the need to grab hold of my ears. It's like she's getting drunker just standing here. "And this whole night, I've been flaunting the forbidden fruit right in your face."

"Oh, it's okay. I hardly noticed. While you were busy flaunting your fruit, Bill and I were going to second on the sofa." *Bad CG, very bad CG!* It's as if I'm an open wound or something—the lies, they just keep pouring out of me like dirty pus. But it's like I said: She won't remember anything in the morning, anyway. And on that note … "Excuse me a sec, would you, sweetie?" I say, freeing myself from her inebriated clutches. "Bill got a little excited while he was kissing the back of my neck, and I need to go make sure he didn't leave any permanent marks."

I hear her jaw hitting the floor as I twist the knob on the bathroom door to check on Sammie. Yeah, I know what I said about the smell of yak, but sometimes—when true friends are involved—you've just gotta suck it up and be a saint.

"Sammie?" I say, shutting the door behind me as I lift my mask. "Are you okay?" *Oh my God, what is she doing?*

"Get out of here!" she yells, lurching forward. Then, in a rush of tears, she falls back against the bathtub. "Damn it. I could've sworn I locked the door."

"Well, you didn't," I say, turning off the faucet. "And I can't unsee what I saw."

Sammie stares at me blankly for a few seconds, her mascara making muddy rivers on her flushed and startled cheeks. "So?" she asks finally. "What do you want to know?"

"Well..." Carefully sidestepping the half-a-dozen plates of food she has lined up on the floor, each one featuring a different, nearly polished-off party snack—from mixed nuts to chocolates to cheese—I kneel down beside her, taking her hand. "I came in and saw you sticking a toothbrush down your throat. I think I already know."

Resting her head on my shoulder, Sammie begins to sob. "It's not as bad as it looks."

"But why?" I ask gently. "*Why* would you do this to yourself?"

She pulls away suddenly, gawking at me as if I'm some kind of brain-dead martian. "Why do you think? You try growing up with a friend like Grace, someone who calls you 'Sasquatch' to your face, someone who thinks you're as oafy and gigantic as Bigfoot."

"Oh, come on, Sammie. You know I'm all for pinning things on Grace, but she didn't do this to you. Grace isn't the one holding you down in front of the can and shoving foreign objects down your gullet."

Sammie smiles reluctantly. "You're right. It *is* me." She pauses to collect her thoughts. "I guess I do it because I'm so miserable."

"And puking your guts up makes you happy?"

"You'd never understand, CG. I'm happy when I'm *bingeing*. And, yeah, letting it all go feels good, too. In a different way. It's like I said," she continues, sniffing as she reaches for a tissue, "you wouldn't understand."

"Then let me help you find someone who *will* understand," I plead. "I'm worried about you, Sammie. I don't want anything bad to happen."

She looks at me strangely, her eyes flashing with unmistakable irritation. "Don't be so dramatic, CG. Discovering my secret doesn't automatically make you the patron saint of bulimic girls. I don't need you to rescue me."

"I'm not trying to be a hero, Sammie. I just care about you, that's all."

"Well, if you care about me, then *trust* me. I'm *fine*." She stands, shaking the crumbs off her nightgown, then offers her hand to help bring me to my feet. "Besides, it's not like I can't control it."

"Does that mean you can stop whenever you want?"

Sammie smiles, straightening her shoulders. "I already have."

"Really?" I ask hopefully, hugging her. I want to believe her. I just . . . don't.

"I promise."

We stay quiet for a while—embracing—until Sammie starts to laugh. "Is it me, or did we just step inside a *Lifetime* movie moment?"

"Totally," I agree, laughing, too. "It doesn't get any more clichéd than two misty-eyed females hugging in the bathroom."

"So, what do you think?" she asks. "Are you willing to let go of me if I swear on your relationship with Bill that I'll never binge and purge again as long as I live?"

"It's a deal," I say, stepping back to study her face, which looks about as sincere as any human face *I've* ever seen. Gandhi and Mother Teresa included. Maybe she really *does* mean it. "Although I've gotta tell you, I think I'm officially over him."

"Why? What happened?"

"I'll fill you in later. For now, let's just say Doctor Love is turning out to be more of a Captain Nebbish." (That's *nerd,* for all my non-Yiddish-speaking companions.)

"Well, that sucks." She giggles. "Let me just clean up in here and I'll be out to survey the damage."

Pulling my little Lone Rangerette disguise back down over my peepers, I bravely reenter the Blind Date from Hell. Only, my monotonous masked man is nowhere to be found. I see Grace with her feet up on the coffee table, nursing a bottle of straight vodka while she flips back and forth between Letterman and Leno on the TV. And, of course, Sleeping Beauty's still passed out in the corner, no doubt dreaming of pretty pink things and doting fathers. But where is Captain Nebbish? Shouldn't he be busy flying around the room spreading boredom in his flaming red cape and green tights? (Okay, make that terry cloth robe and long johns, which he wore specifically to suit our whole lingerie theme ... but same difference.) Could I have really gotten this lucky? Has Humdrum Willy simply disappeared?

"Looking for me?"

*Damn it.* Spoke too soon.

"Uh, yeah," I say, whipping around nervously at the sound of his voice—and crashing nearly smack-dab into his chin. "Oh, sorry," I mumble awkwardly as I lift my head to meet his gaze. And what a gaze it is! We've never stood this close together before and, despite the whole flying nebbish thing, I've gotta admit I'm not hating it. Maybe it's those lips. When they're not rambling a mile a minute about snooze-worthy subjects like ... well, just about everything in his conversational repertoire, they *are* kind of pouty. Sexy. Kissable. *Oh, go ahead, you socially inept, intellectual retard. Lay one on me.*

"I've got to go."

*"Now?"* I ask.

"It's getting late," he says. "And your, uh, troops are weakening out there." He smiles, glancing back at Alona and Grace. "Listen, before I go, I want you to know I understand why you organized this party and I'm okay with the fact that you're not ready to be alone with me yet."

"It's not that I didn't want to see you alone," I tell him. "It's like I explained on the phone . . ." Or like Alona and Grace *instructed* me to explain. "I didn't realize Larmont was so close to Beaubridge. We did a reality shoot in this suite just a few months ago, and the hotel gave my boss some comps which she passed along to me and—"

"I know, I know," he says, wrapping his arms around my waist. Okay, somebody call 911, I'm not kidding—I can physically hear my heart screaming. "And you figured why not make a pajama party out of it and meet me in the process," he continues, resting his hands upon the small of my back as he draws me even closer. "But I know what you were trying to do. I'm on to you."

"Uh . . . you are?"

"Of course I am. And you know something? I really respect you for bringing backup. Whether they were dressed in lingerie or as fully armed guards, the point is that your friends were here in case you got in over your head—which is so important because you can never be too careful, Fiji, especially with Internet dating. You never know *who's* really lurking behind that monitor. Or in this case, that mask."

"Tell me about it."

Bill laughs. "Listen, about this mask business . . . You may not be ready to show me who you are, and that's okay, but . . ." He bashfully lifts his disguise. And can I just say *Whoa?* I forgot that beneath all those nebbishy layers lurked the face of Hunky McHotterson and Sexbomb von Do-me-burg's fully grown love child. I mean, yeah, he's still a dweeb and a sleeping pill and all that, but he's a double dose of boring that sends shivers running throughout parts of my anatomy I didn't even know I had. "I just couldn't leave tonight without showing you who I am."

"Well, I'm glad you did," I admit, soaking in those deep brown eyes, the gentle curves of his boyish face . . . "Because I like what I see."

He grins, leaning down. *Down?* The only time a guy standing this close to you ever leans *down* is if he's about to . . . Oh my God—he *is* about to! I close my eyes, commanding my heart to cease its nervous tremor. My lips begin to part a little as I feel his hands in my hair, his breath drawing closer. This is actually happening: I'm about to make out with my English teacher.

"Oh, this shit is pathetic!" a voice blares from the living room, jolting my eyes wide open. *Okaaaay,* so much for *that* romantic moment. Bill smiles awkwardly as we both turn around in search of the intruder. *Double shit.* Intrusion never looked so good, but I'm in major trouble now.

"Jordan!" I call, waving to *last night's* hookup, who has arrived at this masquerade lingerie shindig in a muscle-hugging sweater and jeans with absolutely no mask to speak of.

He takes one look at me and busts out laughing. "What the hell are you wearing?" Before I can even attempt to explain, his expression turns serious. "You know what, forget I asked. Just *please* tell someone to go throw a blanket over my sister. I didn't come here to puke." He nods toward the six-pack he's carrying. "At least not right away."

"Who is this guy?" Bill asks, his tone undeniably laced with disgust.

"I'm a friend," Jordan says, nodding toward me. "Of *hers.*"

"Is that right?" Bill challenges.

"Well, it's not *wrong.*"

I watch as the hostile undercurrent hisses between them, scorching through their frozen deadlock stare, which could quite possibly go on until I really *am* old enough to get plastered and go to second with a twenty-nine-year-old. Where is Hammerhead Grace when you need her? Or Sammie—what, did she accidentally flush herself down the toilet while she was cleaning up in there?

"Bill," I say finally, hoping to dissolve the tension, though I've gotta admit it's pretty flattering to see the legendary Jordan Spelton acting so possessive over little old me. "This is Jordan, a good friend of mine."

Jordan nods rigidly, then looks at me, vexed. "*This* is Bill? I thought you said you weren't seeing him anymore."

Okay, pause it. Remember how during our first IM chat, I mentioned "my friend Bill" to make Jordan jealous? Well, I sort of ended up telling him that Bill was the older brother of a gal pal back home—hey, I had to give him *some* sense of competition—and that we'd gotten "pretty hot and heavy" until my ex found out and threatened to gut him like an ill-fated fish. I explained that we'd been laying low on account of the whole fillet-of-William thing and said we only talked online now. Oops.

"This is the first time we've gotten together," I tell Jordan, conveniently omitting the word *ever*.

"Hold on a second," Bill says, turning to me. "Fiji, is there something going on between you two I should know about?"

"*Fiji?*" Jordan nearly shouts. "Don't you mean—"

"He means we need a minute alone," I say. *And the*

*crowd goes wild—what a save!* I stare at Jordan pleadingly. "Will you excuse us?"

Shaking his head, Jordan frowns. "And to think I left a *real* party to come spend time with you."

Tell me he didn't just say that. I mean, is this not the role reversal of the century—Jordan Spelton having hurt feelings over a *girl?* Over *me?* As I watch him sulk away into the living room, my heart sinks a thousand stories. I couldn't care less about my saucy little love doctor any-more. Some fantasy *that* turned out to be, right? Hot or not, he'll always be a complete spaz attack in disguise. A total dorkmonger who bores me to tears. The only thing we had going for us was that kiss. And we couldn't even get it off the ground. I say it's time to end this evening from hell and move on to a man who actually knows my name and couldn't possibly bore me if he tried.

"Bill, I have something to tell you ..."

★ ★ ★

I told him Jordan was my ex—ex-husband, that is (has a more adult ring to it, don't you think?)—and that we had a lot of unfinished business to settle before I could be with anyone new. I don't know if he bought my story or not—his face had *confusion* written all over it by the time he left the suite—but I'm just glad it's over. I know

now that Bill wasn't the right guy for me, which is a shame because aside from being physically delectable, he really did give good lesson plan.

"So, should I assume we're sleeping in here?" Jordan asks.

Oh yeah, I guess I should mention that Sammie eventually made it out of the bathroom and ended up crashing on the couch next to a dormant Grace, at which time Jordan and I escaped to the master bedroom, where I helped him get over his hurt feelings.

"We can't *both* sleep in here," I tell him. "What would the others think?"

"CG," he whispers, a funny grin spreading across his face, "have you ever noticed that the others *don't* think? Not unless my sister tells them to, anyway. And believe me, Alona would never do that. Because then *she'd* have to think. And thinking gives my sister vertigo."

I can't help but laugh. "So is that why you like me? Because I'm the only one that thinks?"

"Among other reasons," he says, kissing my forehead. "One of them being how amazing you look in this ridiculous outfit. I think you'd look even more amazing with it off, though." *Admirable segue, buddy, but not a chance.* He gives me a playful smack on the hip. "Take it off and I won't make you explain to me why Bill calls you Fiji." *Oh, shitters . . .*

"Pet name," I say, attempting an innocent smile. "Long story."

"We have all night."

"Not *all* night. I can't sleep in here." Not just because of what the others would think (or not think), but because of the promise I made to myself—that my first time would be special. Strangely enough, this does feel sort of special. Maybe that's the part that scares me. Because I know I'm still not ready. "I just can't."

Jordan seems disappointed, but only momentarily. "Well, then it looks like we'd better make the most of the time we have."

"No complaints out of me."

He draws me closer under the red satin comforter, gearing up for another round of "blinking yellow light"—otherwise known as Proceed with Caution While I Wait to See Just How Far This High School Chick Will Let Me Go Before She Pokes My Eye Out. But there's something on my mind, a question I've been meaning to ask these last six weeks. And I'm especially curious to know the answer now that things have gotten more serious.

"Hey, Jordan, do you love your girlfriend?"

"Oh, Jesus," he says with a tortured groan as he visibly recoils.

"Sorry. Did I just ruin everything?"

He stares up at the ceiling in silence for a long time before answering. "I was prom king," he says finally. "She was prom queen. Our families are friends. Everyone expects us to end up together." Rolling back over to face me, he smiles helplessly. "Does that answer your question?"

"Not really."

Jordan laughs, kissing my nose. "No, I don't love Cassandra. I care about her because I've known her for so long. And I wouldn't want to hurt her. But I don't love her."

"But isn't this—what *we're* doing—isn't *that* hurting her?" Oh, God, what am I saying? *Please, whatever you do, Jordan, don't grow a conscience now.*

"Not if she never finds out."

"But how can you be sure she'll never find out?" I ask. "There have been so many girls . . ." Uh-oh, *waaaaaay* too obvious. I thought I was doing this to feel better about Cassandra. But maybe I just want to feel better about me, to understand what I could possibly mean to a guy who runs around on his girlfriend with a harem of other women, half the time not even knowing their names. I want to understand what was behind his frown tonight when I told him I needed time alone with Bill. I want to know what kind of game we're playing and how long it's going to last.

"There haven't been *that* many girls," he says. "And right now, there's only one."

I smile ... huge. I mean, he is referring to me, right? "I'm glad you cleared that up."

"Anytime. You know, I think about you a lot."

Okay, huge smile just got even huger. "I think about you a lot, too. And I'm glad you came tonight."

"Well, you needed *someone* to save you from that bumbling douche bag," he teases, undoubtedly meaning Bill. "And it's not like any of your friends were going to help, with Grace following in my sister's comatose footsteps and Sammie puking her lungs up in the toilet."

"Wait, how did you know about Sammie?" I ask. "That happened before you even got here."

"Damn, she must have had a *really* rough night, then," Jordan reflects, letting out a little laugh. "All I know is that while you were having your minute alone with *Bill,*" he says, emphasizing the name of his rival, "I tried to use the bathroom, but from the sound of things, Sammie was busy barfing up the state of Pennsylvania in there. So I couldn't get in. I guess she'll think twice before hitting the funny punch bowl next time."

Oh my God ... She lied to me. She can't control it, she hasn't quit, and she's *not* going to be okay. How could I have bought the "I swear I'll never do it again" routine just moments after I caught her gagging on her own

Oral-B? How could I have not realized what was going on before tonight?

"What's the matter?" Jordan asks as his wandering hands come to a grinding halt just shy of my No Trespass Zone. "You want me to stop?"

"No. Whatever you do, don't stop." *Just make me forget what a rotten, miserable person I am, how I've been so caught up in my own drama, I failed to notice the trifling little fact that one of my best friends was slowly killing herself.*

★ ★ ★

"Hey, where are you going?" Grace whispers, popping her head up from the sofa as I scurry across the beige berber carpet in my bare feet. *Shit.* I was hoping to make it from the master suite into the spare bedroom without stirring a single soul. Mission obviously not accomplished.

"To bed," I say quickly.

"Well, where *were* you?"

"Um . . ." Sweet mother of Easter, why does everything have to be so damn complicated? "The bathroom. Sorry if I woke you."

"You didn't," she says plainly. "I've been up for twenty minutes." *Twenty minutes?* How freaking screwed am I? "I was just lying here thinking." *Thinking?* Well, so much for Jordan's theory on *that*.

In the flecks of moonlight that have filtered through the balcony blinds, I see that Grace's face is stained with eye makeup, her hair frizzier than Glory's after a ten-mile hike in a hurricane. It would be a perfect time to tell her she looks like hell. Instead, I say, "I was taking a crap."

"Sorry?"

"That's why I was in the bathroom so long." I mean, hey, there's a time for sparring and a time for coming up with emergency excuses to cover your almost-busted ass.

"You expect me to buy that?" Grace asks, her voice reeking of skepticism. *Uh-oh.* "Don't worry. I won't say anything. I mean, it's *your* life. And God knows you already have enough on me to bury my friendship with Alona," she whispers. She pauses for a second, and in the moonlit darkness I think I actually detect sincerity in her eyes. "I just think you should know . . . he's not as nice as he seems." Ah, sincerity schmincerity. She was probably just holding in a fart or something.

"I don't know what you're talking about," I say, shrugging her off. "I told you I was in the bathroom."

"Okay, fine. I believe you." She *does?*

"You *do?*"

"Sure," Grace says halfheartedly. "Just do me a favor?"

"Anything." *Providing you keep your toxic trap shut and forget this entire conversation come sunrise.*

"Well, wait. First, come with me." Taking my hand, she climbs off the couch and leads me toward the balcony door, sliding it open. "Let's keep talking out here." She guides me onto the platform, where we're instantly hit with a frosty blast of the best March has to offer in late-night winds.

"Don't you think it's a little cold?" I ask. "You could lose a nipple out here."

Grace smiles. "Just don't think about it. Concentrate on the view instead. Isn't it amazing?"

"Actually, yeah." Wait, just a second. Grace Checkov and I actually agree on something? Is anyone writing this down? Has to be a first.

"I love balconies. Every year, I'm forced to go on vacation with my dad, his twelve-year-old wife, and their three evil alien rugrats. But I never care where we go, as long as the room has a balcony. At least then I know I'll be able to get away from them, breathe clean air, maybe even jump if I have to." She laughs, but I've gotta say, I've never seen anyone look so sad. "It's supposed to be some kind of bonding ritual. But really, they just take me with them so my mom and her latest boy toy can get me out of their hair for a week. I guess it's my dad's way of repaying her for the whole *running off with a younger woman and starting a brand-new family* thing."

Damn, no wonder this bitch is so cranky. I'd be, too, if I had a home life like that. Maybe she was right before Maybe my parents and I are living in some nauseatingly wholesome *Waltons* rerun where cheating and eating disorders and absentee fathers don't exist. And if that's the case, *praise the Lord*. I was so captivated by these girls when I first came to Beaubridge—from their attitudes to their bank accounts to their star status in the halls— but I don't even think the promise of perpetual popular- ity could get me to trade places with any of them now.

"Listen," Grace says, turning away from the view to face me, "about that favor ..."

"What is it?" I ask. Here we go. Payback time.

"I know you're enjoying being the sexy new girl on the scene right now."

"Huh?" I giggle doubtfully. "I, um, didn't know that I was."

"Well, whatever. I just want to let you know that it doesn't last forever. One minute you may be hot; the next, you're completely forgotten." She looks down at the ground as the wind whips through her wild auburn curls. "Just don't do anything you'll regret."

"Why are you telling me this?"

Grace raises her head a little, peeking up at me warily. "Look, I know we don't always get along." *Um, try never.* "But that doesn't mean I think you deserve to experience what I've been through. So, just do me a favor and be careful."

"What are you talking about?" I ask. "What have you been through?"

"It's not important," she says, waving me off. "It happened a long time ago."

"What happened? And with who?"

Grace sighs. "You don't know him, CG. It was right after I found out my stepmother was pregnant." She shakes her head, shuddering. "With *triplets.*"

"Oy vey."

"Exactly," she says, laughing softly. "Anyway, I found myself in a situation with this guy—a counselor at my overnight camp—and he paid attention to me. At a time when no one else would."

"When you say 'attention,' you mean . . ."

"We had sex," she says bluntly.

"Are you *serious?*"

"It was no big deal. Well, I mean, *you* know. *You've* done it." Oh, *crapsicles,* I forgot. "The act itself doesn't last long, but the feelings . . ." She smiles sadly. "Well, at least your crazy ex-boyfriend was in love with you. This guy didn't give two shits about me. He was older and he used me, and then he threw me away. And the sick part is, I never got over him. How pathetic is that?"

"It's not. I mean, I never really got over Alex, either."

And there it is: perhaps the only honest thing I've said since I met her.

"Does he know?"

I shake my head. "We don't talk anymore."

"Well, that just proves my point."

"What point?" I ask her.

"That all men are jerks. I mean, for God's sake, CG, if my own *mother* can't handle the way guys treat her after sex, girls our age are definitely too young to be having it."

"But I'm not," I protest. "I mean . . . I'm not anymore."

"Good." She reaches out, tugs on my hair. "Because if anyone's going to make your life hell, it should be me. Not some asshole guy who's never even had the pleasure of hating you."

"Oh yeah?" I ask, shoving her playfully.

"Yeah," she says, and then—without any kind of warning whatsoever—she pulls me close for a hug. "Just promise me you won't be a stupid girl, CG. The world is already full of them."

"I promise," I say, hugging her back. By the way, have I mentioned how *weird* this is?

"And don't ever say anything, either. I never told Alona about the camp counselor because—"

"As long as she's still a virgin, you figure you might as well be one, too?"

"Pretty much," she admits. "But you know, that's what I admire about you—the way you're just your own person all the time, no matter what everyone else is doing. To tell you the truth, I don't know how you find the courage." She pulls back a little, smiles. "But I guess it's why I trust you." *What the funk?* "Because I know you're a bigger person than I am. We're not enemies, CG. An enemy is someone who would run out and use what I've said tonight to turn people against me, and I know you'd never do that."

"You're right. I wouldn't," I assure her as I gaze down over the edge of the balcony, wondering just how much of a jump it could really be. *But do you happen to have a name for someone who'd tell the entire multimillion-user MySpace community that you're a good-for-nothing dope-whore junkie? Oh, wait, I've got one: Dead Meat.*

# twenty blaze of glory

"Hey," I say, peeking my head through Glory's bedroom door. "Your mom said it would be all right to come in."

"So, come in."

Taking a few steps into Glory's room is like taking a ten-year leap back in time. I mean, I know Glory's made the transition from grade school to high school, but let's just say her room is still wearing its training bra. Case in point: the fact that she's sitting here cross-legged on her SpongeBob Squarepants bedspread cuddling her childhood Tickle Me Elmo doll. Is it any wonder why someone as insecure as Grace broke away from her? Then again, who am I to talk about being insecure? Everybody's favorite rebel, and I was afraid to even come here today.

"What's up?" she asks.

"Um..." I know if I ever want to smooth things over between Glory and Sammie, I've got to mention the crank call, but the coward in me is hoping to put off the inevitable. Because I can't think of any rational way to defend Sammie's crime without going into full detail about the way Grace heckled her on the weight issue and ultimately pushed her into the dare. And the more details I provide, the harder it will be to hide the fact that I was there. And if Glory knows I was there...Well, you get the picture. "I just wanted to wish you a happy Easter."

"Said one Jew to another."

"Oh yeah." *Der.* This is gonna be harder than I thought. I mean, she's gotta know they *told* me about it. That's why she's being so curt—she's trying to punish me for my poor taste in friends. But to know I was actually a part of the whole thing? Uh-uh, honey. For now, I think it's definitely safe to say that avoidance is a girl's best friend...Okay, Operation Procrastination, take two. "Actually, I'm just dying to tell you about what happened to me last night."

*Okaaaay,* no reaction. This could be bad. *Just don't let it throw you. Remember, if you act guilty, you* are *guilty, so just keep up the merry moron routine. Shouldn't be* too *much of a stretch.*

"Fiji and Bill finally had their first date!" I blurt excitedly, flopping down next to her on the bed. "And, oh my God, Glory, it was a freakin' disaster! I really could have used your help."

"Why is that?" she asks dryly.

"Well, for starters, Jordan showed up, and you're the only one who knows I've been seeing him." Actually, she knew we were seeing each other before *he* did. And to this day, she thinks I call him my boyfriend. But what can I say? When you start out weaving webs, your life just gets sort of tangled.

Glory shakes her head, baffled. "What was Jordan doing on your date? Come to think of it, what are *you* doing dating guys you meet on the Internet—let alone teachers from our school—when you're already with the so-called man of your dreams?" *And now, ladies and gentlemen, a word from my conscience . . .*

"It's complicated," I tell her.

"Nothing like pointing out the obvious."

"Well, what do you want me to say?" I ask, beginning to crack under the pressure of her superior logic. "I've been stupid. Jordan was there because Bill and I agreed to meet at some stupid party, which Jordan ended up crashing, which made the whole thing with Bill just seem even stupider . . ." I stop to sigh. Why is she staring at me like that? "I don't know what I was doing getting involved with my twenty-nine-year-old English teacher in the first place." And that's the truth.

"I thought you said he was thirty." *Fuuuuuuuck!* Fuck big, giant tiger balls.

"Oh, well, uh . . ." I can't believe this. That lie was so white, it was practically albino. And I only told it to make the whole thing sound more exciting, to rope her in with a little extra relish. Only now that relish has come back to bite me in the ass. Hard. "That must've been because *he* said he was thirty. You know how the older generation is. Once you hit twenty-five, it's all downhill. Everyone just starts rounding up."

"If that's true, then why does every adult *I* know want to sound as young as they can for as long as they can? My mom is thirty-nine and never tells anyone she's forty. As far as I can see, it's *our* generation that's rushing to grow up faster than time moves—case in point, people like you. Adults are always trying to turn back the clock, and believe me, I've never heard of a twenty-nine-year-old wishing they were thirty."

"Yeah, maybe so, but . . ." She's right. The girl with the SpongeBob blanket and *101 Dalmatians* wallpaper has just cornered me with her infinite wisdom, and I have no idea what to say.

"You know what, CG? Just save it, okay?"

My God, she really isn't gonna let this go. "Look, I'm sorry if I forgot to tell you Bill's true age. If I knew it was this important——"

"You'd have created a better lie to cover up the one that just backfired on you," she snaps, flinging her Elmo doll onto the bed as she stands up and stalks across the room. *Damn.* I had no idea the girl was this combustible. *Well, my friends, it was nice knowing you, but it looks like I'm about to go down in a blaze of Glory.* "You know," she says, spinning around, her pasty cheeks flaming a fiery coral, "I'm beginning to think there are a lot of things you 'forget' to tell me."

Gulp.

"Like, where were you Thursday night when Samara decided to humiliate me with that bogus newspaper interview?" she asks.

"I . . . I'm . . ." I'm *crying. Oh,* nice *going, tough girl. Way to look innocent.*

"Let me guess. You're sorry. You didn't mean to hurt anyone—least of all, me—but once things got started, you just didn't know how to stop them. I mean, it was just a silly game, right? A funny crank call in the middle of the night? And let's face it, standing up for me would've meant admitting to Grace and Alona that we were friends. I should've known you'd never have the guts to do that."

She puts her hands on her hips, shaking her head. "You can sit there and cry all you want, CG. It doesn't make a difference. Where were *you* when I was sobbing *my* eyes out the other night? When, like a complete bonehead, I called your house at a quarter to one in the morning hoping you'd be there to console *me?*"

"You called?" I ask, my voice shrill and quaky. "I never got the message."

"Maybe because your mom was half asleep when she answered, but, you know, somehow I managed to glean the words 'slumber party at Alona's' from her slurred response." She walks over to her desk, still decorated with old Powerpuff Girls and Teletubbies stickers, and slumps down in the chair, staring at her knees. "Part of me suspected you were in on it. I was just hoping . . ." She trails off sadly.

"What?"

She glances up at me, her face filled with regret. "That what I'd believed in all that time—our friendship—wasn't fake, that you weren't fake. But I should've known it was too good to be true."

"It wasn't! We *are* friends." And I *am* fake. I realize that now more than ever.

"Oh, come on, look at me, CG," she says. "I know I'm not cool. It's no wonder you tried to keep our 'sisterhood' under wraps around your crew. And hey, I played my part, didn't I? I never once tried to sit at your precious lunch table or tag along on one of your shopping sprees. I was content to stick to my kind and let you keep to yours because you know what, hey, that's high school. And the payback was that after hours, I thought I'd met a really genuine person I could trust. Now that that's gone, what's the use of even talking anymore?"

"Because we have fun together," I say pleadingly, "and I like you. You're the only girl I've met since I moved here who isn't constantly performing to impress other people."

Glory laughs. "Ha! As if *you're* one to talk. You know, I always knew Samara was weak, but I expected more from you."

"And I'm sorry," I apologize, rising from the bed. "I don't know what else I can say."

"There isn't anything more to say. What's done is done." She sighs, gazing down at the floor. "I just can't believe I was dumb enough to think Samara and I were actually getting close again."

"You were," I tell her. "We *all* were. Trust me, Sammie didn't want to make that call any more than I wanted her to make it."

"Trust *you?*" She laughs again, looking up at me. "I think I'd rather take my chances in a lion's den."

"Well, then, help me."

"*Help* you?"

"Glory, I'm in way over my head. Something else happened last night at that party with Jordan and Bill, and I don't know where else to turn."

"This should be good," she says, folding her arms across her chest. "Wait, let me guess. You met *another* older man, this time on the *moon,* and decided to ditch Bachelors One and Two to go get hitched in Vegas. And now you're trying to have the whole thing annulled so you can beat Britney's fifty-five-hour record from 2004."

Hmm. Sounds like something my unstable brain would've cooked up, but unfortunately, in this case, the truth is even more disturbing. I take a deep breath, straightening my shoulders. *Oh, God, please tell me I'm doing the right thing . . .*

"I found out Sammie's bulimic."

"What?" she asks, her eyes widening. "How?"

"I walked in on her yakking in the bathroom surrounded by half a dozen plates of food. She was using a toothbrush to force the puke out."

"Oh, Jesus," she despairs, wringing her hands. "What did she say?"

"That it's no big deal and she's able to control it. But I know she was lying."

"Well, *of course* she was lying," Glory retorts, visibly distraught. "Bulimia's a disease. You can't *control* a disease.

She needs help." We're both quiet for a few seconds while Glory regains her composure. "I'll take care of this," she says finally . . . calmly. "Just do one thing for me, okay?"

"Anything," I say, feeling grateful. Not to mention relieved. See, I knew I could count on good old Glory. Not only is she willing to help Sammie, but she's probably rethinking her hostile contempt for me right as we speak. It's only a matter of time before I'm forgiven. "I'll do anything you want. You just name it."

"Get the hell out of my house."

# twenty-one the day the world turned rebel chic

Have you ever had the sneaking suspicion that the world was playing a trick on you? That God and the angels and all your dead relatives were up there with a big barrel of popcorn laughing their asses off while they watched you get punked on some giant satellite screen in the clouds? Well, I think it's happening to me. Today is our first day back at school since Easter break, and let's just say that if acting freaky were the latest trend, the whole student body would be in style. People have been whispering, staring, pointing, offering me their congratulations as well as their condolences. What's going on is far beyond *this* girl's guess, and with Sammie out sick and Glory no longer speaking to my sorry ass, I have nowhere to turn for a reality check. Of course, there's always Alona, but Her Majesty may just be the freakiest thing I've seen yet. When I first caught sight of her this morning in homeroom, I wondered who had wheeled in the full-length mirror. Because if I wasn't staring directly into my own reflection—or hallucinating from a bad batch of Corn Flakes—then I'd just met my latest competition: a brand-new "new girl" with poker-straight hair, baggy corduroys, chunky black shoes, and an oversized hoodie. Imagine my shock when I realized this mini me was actually Miss Teen Vogue America sans miniskirt, diamonds, heels, and amber waves. I haven't had a chance to ask her about the extreme makeover yet, but what is lunchtime for if not to dish?

"Hey!" I yell cheerily, waving her down amid the hustle and bustle of the cafeteria mob. "Looking for me?"

Alona smiles thankfully. At least, I *think* that's her beneath that big barrage of camouflage. (Did I mention she's also rocking the earth tones? What happened to all that *pink?*) "How's it going?" she asks, taking a seat across from me at our usual table.

"Strange," I admit.

"Strange?"

"I swear to Christ!" Grace bellows, approaching us from my right. "This has got to be the worst day I've ever lived through!" As she parks herself next to Alona, I can't help but notice: They're both wearing the same clothes. They're both wearing *my* clothes.

"Oh, not you, too!" I blurt, surveying her new look. For one thing, those artificially straightened curls have *got* to go. We're talking one of the most atrocious hair don'ts since Lindsay Lohan's first brush with blond back in 2005. And that was pretty damn tragic.

"What do you mean, oh, not me, too?" Grace asks. "Are you having a shitty day also?"

"Not shitty so much as *bizarre*," I clarify.

"Strange," Alona supplies, reminding me of where we were when Grace's laid-back twin blustered in swearing to Christ.

"Right," I agree. "The strangest." They both stare at me curiously, wide-eyed and innocent, awaiting my explanation with their heads perched together like a pair of dumbstruck dodo birds. *Oy vey.* This really is *The Twilight Zone.* "For starters," I begin tentatively, "what's with the outfits?"

"What do you mean?" Alona asks blankly. Grace nudges her, smiling. "Oh, right!" she gushes, and then they both beam at me.

"I don't get it," I confess.

Grace raises one eyebrow theatrically. "We call it 'rebel chic.'" *Say what?*

"See, Grace told me Sammie was just being flip the other night," Alona explains, taking over. "You know, when she said everyone was dressing like you now? But I got to thinking, if everyone *isn't* doing the rebel chic, they totally should be! I mean, CG, your look is just so inspired."

"Inspired?" I repeat.

"You know, like, off the beaten path," she says. "Unconventional, uninhibited, reckless. It's like you're good enough to be a Four Top but have stayed true to your roots or something—like one of those Hollywood celebs who refuses to go all red-carpet glam because deep down, she's just a wholesome old country girl at heart." *Yup, that's me, wholesome as a haystack in Texas.* "Anyway, I figured it was time to shake things up a bit." She grins, her eyes twinkling like a pair of brilliant blue sapphires glistening under a bright sunny sky. "You know, start a revolution based on comfort and . . . What were the other things, Grace?"

"Individuality and freedom of expression," Grace provides as she roots through her lunch tote. "And with Alona and me dressing the part, it's just a matter of days before the whole world turns rebel chic."

So, wait, let me see if I've got this straight. As part of her ongoing quest to heal Mother Earth, Alona has decided to grant all Beaubridge gals the freedom to express their "individuality" by cloning themselves after *me?*

"How much fun is that?" Alona squeals.

"Oodles," I tell her. "But don't you miss your old clothes?"

"Are you kidding?" she asks. "My feet have never felt better, and would you believe I'm not even wearing a bra today?" Her face suddenly fills with excitement as she reaches down to yank on her sweatshirt zipper. "Check it out."

"No, it's okay!" I protest, scrunching my eyes closed. "I'll take your word for it. Sometimes I don't wear a bra, either."

Alona giggles. "No, silly. I mean you have to see this."

I open my peepers to behold her and Grace stretching their hoodies wide open, flashing me their . . . *Janis Joplin T-shirts?*

"Since when do you two listen to Janis?" I ask.

They glance at each other, exchanging smiles. "Since yesterday," Grace says proudly. "And what a set of pipes."

"Oh, and check these out," Alona tells me, lifting her sleeve. Grace follows suit until they've both revealed the hidden surprises on their right wrists. "See," Alona gushes, "they're just like the woven fabric bracelet *you* wear!" *If this isn't a joke, please shoot me.* If Alex only knew how the symbol of our former friendship was being exploited by these two fluffheads, he'd crap his pants in a fit of disgust and FedEx the turds to their doorsteps. Or maybe I'm just flattering myself. I mean, with our friendship dead and buried, he may not even give a shit (pun totally intended).

"Oh, wow, cool bracelets," says a voice to my left. We all turn to see Kara Fargus, the real eyes and ears of our school paper, salivating at us from behind her tortoiseshell rims. Notoriously nosy, this future Katie Couric is known for only sucking up when she wants the scoop.

"Thank you, Ms. Editor," Alona says coyly. "And if you're looking to stay one step ahead of the news, you may want to print a little blurb in this week's issue of the *Beat* about a fashion trend that will soon be taking the school by storm."

"Great," Kara responds matter-of-factly, "but in the meantime, I was hoping you ladies might have the skinny on your friend Sammie Fleischer."

"What about her?" I ask.

"Well, inside sources tell me she'll be out for at least a month. Apparently, her parents shipped her off to some rehabilitation center in California for 'treatment,'" Kara says, making little quotation marks with her fingers.

Holy shit. Glory kept her word: She took care of it. And now, the unforeseen consequence of doing the right thing—the fact that Sammie's about to become fodder for the high school gossip mill.

"The question is, what's her problem?" Kara asks, cocking her head suspiciously.

"Her problem?" I echo. Fuck fodder. They're not gonna squeeze any pulp out of this story, not so long as I can help it. "Maybe it's you!"

"Sorry?" she asks, her fluttering lashes betraying her polished reporter's stance. "I just thought that as her closest confidantes, you might want to get the truth out."

"The truth is, you'd better beat it," I tell her, "while your tongue is still attached to your mouth."

Grace stifles a giggle as Kara stalks off in a huff.

"Wow," Alona says, sighing. "That was pretty amazing. They didn't name a fashion trend after you for nothing." She smiles softly. "But just remember, CG, the media is your friend." I stare at her, baffled. Isn't she worried about Sammie? *At all?*

"Yeah," I say. "Sorry. I'll work to modify my behavior." A long bout of silence passes as we all focus on our respective lunches. I notice that Grace's afternoon meal consists of a jumbo bag of Doritos, a king-size Hershey's bar, and a can of nondiet soda. Sheesh. Either Aunt Flo has stopped in for one brutal visit or this really is the worst day she's ever lived through. "Hey, Grace," I say finally, setting my PB&J down on its aluminum-foil wrapper. "Anything wrong?" *Aside from the fact that one of your "closest confidantes" has been mysteriously shipped to some rehab center three thousand miles away?*

Grace glances up at a nearby flock of jocks, all of

whom happen to be leering in this very direction with lecherous, hungry smiles glued to their dopey faces. When they catch her looking, one of them begins to laugh. Another holds a dollar bill out in front of him, waving it suggestively. "How about a quickie?" he asks. "How much do you charge for that?"

Holy crapola—the MySpace thing! I've been so preoccupied these last few days—from worrying about Sammie... to mourning the loss of Glory... to moving full-steam ahead in my undefined relationship with Jordan, who's been IM-ing me like a fiend ever since our down 'n dirty penthouse romp (which, just so you know, did not change things in the "white wedding" department)—I completely forgot I was a dead woman!

Grace groans, snapping off a piece of her chocolate bar. "See that?" she says, turning to me. "I've been dealing with comments like that all day. And all because I apparently posted a blog on MySpace claiming to be some kind of high-class crack whore. Or something to that effect."

"Well, why would you go and do that?" Alona asks innocently.

"I *didn't*," Grace says, seething through her clenched smile. "That's the point."

"So, you're saying someone hacked into your account and posted all that crazy crap, *pretending* to be you?" I ask.

*Please, God, just let me get away with this one and I'll never ask another favor of you ever again. As long as I live.* "Who would do such a thing?"

Grace shrugs. "There are tons of haters out there, CG. I mean, just because I'm popular doesn't mean people like me."

"Of *course* people like you," Alona tells her. "*I* like you."

"Thanks, Lonnie," Grace says, forcing a grateful grin. "But *somebody* despised me enough to slam my name all over the Internet. Monica McKinney says the blog has been up since Friday morning, sometime around a quarter to four. I haven't logged on in days or you can bet I'd have deleted that malicious smear campaign by now." She tosses her candy bar down on the table, crossing her arms. "There's nothing worse than bad press. I swear, now I understand how Courtney Love feels."

"Wait, just hold on," Alona says calmly. "You were at *my* house Friday morning. We were sleeping by a quarter to four. You know everybody listens to me. I'll just tell them you couldn't have written the blog."

"But who *did?*" Grace asks, begging to know. "That's what I need to find out."

"Hey, you guys," I interrupt, "not to change the subject . . ." *Even though that's* exactly *what I'm trying to do.* "But do you think Sammie's gonna be okay?"

Alona smiles wistfully. "I don't know. I hope so. But I don't really understand this whole treatment thing. She never told us about any kind of serious problem."

"Well, maybe she couldn't. I mean, maybe it was too hard to talk about," I say. "Maybe she didn't even know she had a problem."

"I *always* know when I have problems," Alona points out.

"Well, maybe her problems were ... deeper," I conclude, biting my lower lip.

"You mean, like, gambling?" Alona asks.

"Uh, not exactly," I say.

"That's *it!*" Grace exclaims, slamming her fist down onto her Doritos bag, which responds with a loud, resounding *cruuuunch*. "It was Sammie!" Her eyes narrow into angry little slits as her chest heaves up and down, her breath quickening while she talks. "It makes perfect sense. We all know how much she hated me for asking about her weight and then daring her to make that crank call. In fact," she says, pausing to connect the dots in her mind, "I logged on to my homepage right in front of her that night while we were arguing. And I don't think I remembered to sign off before we went to bed. She could've easily posted the blog after I fell asleep."

"Do you really think Sammie would do that?" Alona asks, dipping a slice of fresh baguette into her pâté. "And just before she went into rehab?"

Grace shrugs, seemingly satisfied with her new theory. "Well, it did make for the perfect hit and run. Not to mention that nobody had a better motive. I mean, seriously, who had it in for me worse than Sammie?" *Don't say it . . .*

"Nobody I can think of." Oh, dear God, I said it! Have I really just sunken so low as to blame my bulimic best friend for my odious act of false bloggery? "But considering how much she's been through, I wouldn't really hold it against her." Better?

"Easy for you to say," Grace whines. "You had nothing to do with this obscene little scheme."

"Well, *that's* true," I concede. Okay, so I made a scapegoat out of Sammie, and as punishment, I'll say it fast five times while walking backwards, blindfolded, through a cornfield stark raving naked in the middle of the night. Sound good? I mean, it's not like I *ruined* her or anything. Sammie can always deny her involvement when she gets out of rehab next month. Hell, she may not even have to—months in high school pass like dog years. By the time Sammie gets back, Grace probably won't even remember what happened.

"I'll never forget this," the alleged crack whore vows, shoving a fistful of Dorito crumbs into her mouth. Well, so much for *that*.

"What do you guys think Sammie's in rehab for?" Alona asks pleasantly. *Pleasantly?* This *is* our friend's well-being we're talking about, right? Not the latest celebrity meltdown. Which leads me to my next point: Where *did* Her Holy Highness learn to prioritize? I mean, on one hand, she's this major philanthropist, hard at work trying to save the world from high heels, underwires, excess syllables, and other known evils. And yet, when it comes to the welfare of her friends, she's about as deep as a toilet bowl.

"Who knows?" Grace says dryly. "Maybe it's OA— Overtanners Anonymous." Alona giggles.

"Or SA," Grace muses. "Sasquatches Anonymous."

"Grace, come on!" I demand. "Show a little respect for the, uh . . . *rehabilitating*."

Alona clears her throat, embarrassed.

"Like the kind of respect she showed me?" Grace snaps. "CG, you don't know the looks I've been getting all day."

"Can't be any stranger than the looks *I've* been getting," I tell her. "And I don't even have a MySpace account."

"Well . . . that's my fault," Alona says quietly. "I've sort of been bragging about you. If people are looking at you strangely, it's only because they want to talk to you but don't know quite what to say. Believe me, CG, they're all just as shocked as I am."

"Shocked about what?"

An enormous smile overwhelms her face as she rises to her feet, circles the table, and plunks down into the empty chair beside me. "I had no idea you were an alcoholic!" she blurts, suffocating me with a big, syrupy bear hug.

"I . . ." Oh, fucknuggets. What am I gonna do now?

"Sorry," Grace mouths silently, holding her hands out in front of her like a guilty child. Then, out loud, she asks, "It wasn't a secret, was it?" *No, you were just drunk as piss when I told you that story. You weren't supposed to remember a thing.*

"Oh, don't be mad at her for telling me," Alona says, pulling back a little to look at my face. "She was just so amazed at all you'd been through. And so am I. I mean, ten months' sobriety!" she squeals. "How awesome is that?"

*You've gotta be shitting me.* The whispers, the stares, the congratulations, the condolences—it was all because even with a belly full of vodka, Hammerhead Grace still has a memory like Rain Man? Because she told Alona, and Alona told the world, that I was a recovering rummy? And now that world thinks I'm some sort of hero? I haven't a clue what to say.

"I'm speechless."

Alona laughs. "Well, you'd better get over that by this afternoon!"

"Why?" I ask. "What's this afternoon?"

She takes a deep breath, her face lighting up with pride. "Well, your story got me thinking and I talked to some faculty types... and would you believe this school has never had an alcohol and drug awareness group? I mean, can you imagine?" She grins, fanning herself excitedly. "But starting today, that all changes. We'll meet once a week in the auditorium. And guess who our club president is going to be?"

Uh, how about I just spare us all and jump off a moving bus?

★ ★ ★

You wouldn't believe how many of today's young people, just in Beaubridge alone, are interested in drugs and alcohol. In *fighting* them, I mean. That really is what I meant to say. I'm just anxious. Make that a sniveling basketcase. With gas. Not funky, foul-smelling fart gas, but the kind that fills your stomach with buckets of nerves just moments before that doctor's office door swings open, or the teacher calls you to the front of the room to make your dreaded oral presentation. Or Alona Spelton welcomes all 155 of your peers to the first weekly meeting of the Beaubridge High School Drug and Alcohol Awareness Group.

"... or DAAG, as we shall from hereon refer to it. The second A is silent," Alona says gleefully as she stands behind the podium on the auditorium stage, speaking into a long, skinny microphone. "This is an amazing turnout, so I want to thank all of you for coming. Hopefully, with your continued support, we can work together to discuss issues that are important to us all, despite whatever individual differences we may have."

Is it just me, or is she completely in her element up there? If I didn't know better, I'd swear I was watching one of the Bush twins deliver Daddy's State of the Union address. No wonder I'm about to be sick.

"But before we begin outlining our goals and plans for the future, there is someone I'd like you to meet." *Oh, God.* "She's not only a very special friend of mine, but she's also your club president. And she's here today to tell you her story. So, please put your hands together and make some noise for CG Silverman!" That would be my cue . . .

I rise to my feet as the cheers soar around me. "CG! CG! CG!" God, they really do obey her every word, don't they? Can you believe they're actually chanting my name? You'd think I was freakin' Donovan McNabb or something! I mean, since when do teenage booze-hounds get treated like stadium champions?

Alona is waiting for me up on the stage. She takes my hands, leading me over to the podium. It's now or never and, looking out into that sea of expectant faces, I know the time has come. There's no way I can turn back. My public is demanding a speech.

"Hello," I say, speaking carefully into the microphone as the crowd falls silent. "My name is CG Silverman and I'm an alcoholic ..."

# twenty-two another one bites the dust

Tell me the truth. Am I starting to smell? Believe me, when your nearest and dearest start dropping like flies, it's a question you've gotta ask. And it's no secret that my circle of friends has recently gotten smaller than a microscopic mouse turd. First, there was Alex, then Glory, and now my latest casualty, which blew in from the Left Coast last night without any warning at all and knocked me so hard on my ass I don't think I'll be sitting for a week.

It all started when I phoned Sammie's house to ask for her digits in rehab. Mrs. Fleischer, who seemed more than happy to hear from me, obligingly provided the number for the Douglas Center for Eating Disorders in Santa Monica. Now, if only I hadn't made the unfortunate mistake of calling there . . .

"Douglas Center, how may I help you?" the receptionist answered.

"Hi. I was wondering if I could speak to a patient of yours. Samara Fleischer?"

"May I ask who's calling?"

"CG Silverman."

"One moment, please. I'll see if that patient's available." About a year and a day later, she returned. "I'm sorry. Ms. Fleischer can't come to the phone right now."

"Okay," I said. "Do you know of a better time for me to reach her?"

"I'm not familiar with her schedule, ma'am." *Ma'am?*

"Okay, well then could you just tell her I called?"

"This is a two-hundred-patient facility, ma'am. We don't deliver personal messages." Again with the *ma'am*. And why was she being so snarky?

"Well, uh, okay," I bumbled. "I guess I'll just call back a little later."

"I wouldn't bother. I'm sorry to be so blunt. But Samara Fleischer made it clear that she does *not* wish to speak to you." *Ouch*. And I thought going to the orthodontist stung like a bitch.

Not that Sammie doesn't have the right to hate me just a little. I mean, if Glory's responsible for her sudden westward migration, she must've figured out *I* was the one who spilled the proverbial beans by now. But what are beans compared with saving lives?

★ ★ ★

"So, have you heard anything from our mystery blogger?" Grace asks as she leafs through Upton Sinclair's *The Jungle,* jotting down notes for one of Bill's terminally tedious study guides. Yes, here we are again—muddling through our extra-credit purgatory while my former flame attends a staff meeting down the hall.

"Oh, you mean Sammie?" I ask. And yes, I realize I'm still impeaching the innocent for my own abominable violation of justice, but if Grace would simply stop mentioning it, I'd be able to stop laying blame.

"No," she says sarcastically. "The *other* raving asshole who hijacked my blog last weekend." She flashes a playful smile. "Of course I mean Sammie."

I shake my head. "No, I haven't heard from her. But I talked to her mom last night. She said the place where Sammie's staying doesn't even allow phone calls. She wouldn't tell me what kind of place it is, though." Pretty good cover, huh? If I do say so myself.

"Hmm," Grace reflects. "This whole thing is just beyond me. I mean, Sammie's always been such a simple person. Who would've guessed she had problems?" Question: Is calling someone "simple" ever *not* an insult?

"Well, you can't judge a book by its cover," I philosophize as I take a moment to assess Grace's latest duds. Oh, and by the way, Alona was right—it *is* a revolution. In just two days, nearly half the school has gone rebel chic. "I mean, look how perfect Bill seemed on the outside, but once he revealed his true colors . . ." I trail off, shrugging helplessly.

Grace gives me a knowing smile. "Say no more," she groans, clearly recalling today's lunchtime tale of the dangerous masked man who nearly talked me to death at the ball. "Ick. But at least you got some good action off of him."

You know, I think I liked it better when Grace and I were clawing each other's eyes out. Before our little balcony bonding session, when I was still blind as a bat to her troubled past and had never attempted to test her drunken memory with stories about alcoholism and going to second base with our English teacher. Yes, those were the days. Now she's just another friend I've lied to, another part of the circle waiting to snap off and make the mouse turd even smaller.

"Yeah, but what's action, really?" I ask. "I mean, if the person you're getting the action *from* is dull enough to beat Kenny G in a Battle of the Bores?"

"But there's no denying how cute he is."

"Who, Kenny G?" I tease, and Grace giggles. "Honestly, I don't even care how cute Bill is. Fiji is never calling him again. What's that saying? Bore me once, shame on you. Bore me twice, I'm an effing moron for not learning my lesson the first time?"

She laughs, shrugging her shoulders.

"All I know is that it was fun while it lasted. I mean, it's not every day a girl gets to have an online affair with her dead-sexy English teacher," I say. "It's just that life is short, you know? I can't be Fiji forever, especially after that date from—"

"*Hell-ooo,* Mr. Fenowitz!" Grace suddenly cheers, drowning out my reference to Satan's inferno. Of course, she's kidding, though, right? I mean, the man in question couldn't possibly be ...

Standing right behind me. With smoke coming out of his ears.

*Oh ... Oh my God ... Oh my Satan ... I've definitely done it now.*

Just make sure my parents know I love them, all right? Because something tells me I won't be making it out of this classroom alive. The final words on my tombstone? What else? *She didn't mean it.* That should get me off the hook with just about everyone I've enraged. I mean, they've gotta feel *some* sympathy toward me once I'm six feet under.

"Grace," Bill says, nodding curtly. "You're excused for the afternoon. I need to speak with CG in private." *Oh, heaven, help me...HELP ME!* "If you wouldn't mind closing the door on your way out?"

Yup, I'm definitely a goner.

Faster than a speeding bullet, Grace gathers her things and disappears behind the heavy wooden door. *Shit. Fuck. Fart. Balls. Lizard dick* ... We're *alone*. And silence never sounded so loud.

Bill crosses the room and stands behind his desk—arms folded, nostrils flared, jaw clenched tighter than my father's wallet the last time I asked for a twenty. I'm no body language expert, but these can't be good signs. "So, you're Fiji?" he finally barks.

I nod, not saying anything. I mean, hey, I watch TV. I know I have the right to remain silent.

"And this," he says, signaling back and forth between us. "You and me. What was that? Just some kind of high school prank?" He shakes his head. "Must've been pretty funny. Sitting there with all your spoiled-brat friends, making fun of the miserable, lonely teacher who can't get a date."

"It wasn't like that at all!" I protest. I know everything I say can and will be used against me, but this is too important. Fiji may have been a hoax, but I can't have him thinking the worst of her. Or of me. "I . . . I cared about you."

"*Cared* about me?" he yells, slamming his hands down on his desk. "You're a kid! You don't know what it means to care about someone! To actually have a reason to feel excited about life again! To tell your mother she can stop worrying because you've finally met someone nice, and at the same time know how pathetic you sound, seeing as this 'nice girl'—who might seriously be the One—is just some random person you bumped into online." He sighs heavily, slumping back against the chalkboard. "Some figment of your delusional imagination." My God, he told *his mother* about me?

"Look, I'm sorry," I say. "I never meant for things to get so out of hand."

"*Sorry?* All you can say is *sorry?*" He stares at me incredulously, his eyes bulging forth from their sockets. "CG, I almost *kissed* you!"

"I know," I admit, trying not to smile at the memory, which despite everything still goes down in *her*story as my best almost-kiss ever.

"And you realize I could lose my job for that?"

"But nothing happened," I remind him.

"*Nothing happened?*" he repeats, completely flabber-

gasted. "What about the fact that I spent the night party-
ing in a hotel room with three teenage girls?"

"Yeah, but you didn't know it at the time. We told
you we were twenty-five."

"Right," he says abruptly. "Tell that to the judge. You
know, you deserve the punishment here, CG, not me.
But the irony is, I can't even write you up for this. Because *I'm* the one they'll come after. And I'm not just
talking about getting fired from your precious little sub-
urban high school. I could lose my teaching license—for
good—and never be allowed to practice my profession
anywhere, ever again! *Then* what would I do with my
life, huh?" He lets out a short, heavy sigh, shaking his
head in frustration. "Damn it, CG, don't you understand
what you've done? It doesn't matter whether I'm guilty
or innocent—whether I *knowingly* entered the shark-
infested waters or not. The point is, I entered. And even
if the law were capable of making that distinction, the
public wouldn't be so forgiving. An educator's reputation doesn't just bounce back after a scandal like this. If
word ever got out, no parent in their right mind would
let me within a hundred yards of their kid. And who
could blame them? So, see, it's just better to pretend this
whole thing never happened, because making you pay
for your crime would be a sure-fire road to career sui-

cide." He takes a seat at his desk, burying his head in his hands. "You can go now."

"You mean, that's it?" I ask shakily. "We're done?"

"Congratulations, CG," he says, glancing up at me, his face red and agitated. And sad. He's gonna miss her, isn't he? The exotic island girl who in just six short weeks had him believing she was the One. "You got off scot-free."

If that's the case, then why do I feel like I've just been burned at the stake?

# twenty-three untitled

Ladies and gentlemen, we interrupt your regularly scheduled program to bring you this special news bulletin: Jordan Spelton will be returning to Beaubridge next weekend! Word broke just moments ago as he and his young (but strikingly mature) ... er ... "companion" chatted via instant messenger on their respective PCs.

In other affairs, all is quiet on the home front. In the days following the unexpected showdown between high school Honors English teacher Bill Fenowitz and sophomore prodigy CG Silverman, both parties remain civil yet distant. And though still estranged from former allies Fleischer and Finklefuss, Silverman says she has not completely lost hope. In a statement issued to her publicist, the sage beauty reveals, "In a world where the generous hands of fate continue to reunite

*starcrossed lovers like Mr. Spelton and myself, I refuse
to give up on my friends."*

*This concludes our broadcast. We now return you to
your regularly scheduled program, already in progress.*

★ ★ ★

Okay, so maybe I don't exactly have a future in TV journalism, but can you blame me for getting a little ahead
of myself? After all the drama I've endured this past
week—being dropped by my two closest friends in the
world *and* coming to terms with the fact that I nearly
destroyed a man's life—this news about Jordan's surprise
homecoming is nothing if not a sweet escape. You can't
imagine how lonely I've been without Glory and Sammie. And the worst part is, they don't even know how
much they mean to me. And now they probably never
will. It's the same with Bill. I mean, yeah, the whole Fiji
thing was sort of a blast while it lasted, but it was never
just a game to me. The awkwardness factor—as I sit there
in class every day trying to pretend we've never known
each other as anything more than teacher and student—
is beyond excruciating. But even more painful is the
hurt that lurks behind his sunken brown eyes. I know it's
there, because I feel it, too. I'm just not sure how I can
make amends—with any of them. Neither Sammie nor

Glory will take my calls, and Bill . . . well . . . I've composed about a half a dozen apology e-mails to him since our confrontation that day after school, but nothing I say seems to come out right—there's no justification for what I did; no reasonable explanation for treating a poor, innocent man so badly, for never once stopping to consider his feelings at all—so I've deleted every draft. He may never know how sorry I am—and neither may Sammie or Glory—but the worst part of all this is Alex. Like the proverbial angel on my shoulder, all I can see is him sitting there, shaking his head in disappointment over what I've become, mourning the loss of the girl he once called his friend—a girl who would never hurt people the way I have lately. Wondering if he ever really knew me at all.

With everything that's happened and all the misery I've caused, I realize I don't exactly deserve to have fun right now. But not everyone gets what they deserve. And some people get more. God is obviously spoiling me rotten with Jordan, but I guess I'm just too weak to resist. Would *you* be able to? I didn't think so. Anyway, back to my breaking news . . .

It started out just like any other routine chat session, with Jordan emerging from the cybershadows to serve up my daily dose of casual no-strings-attached flirtation. I wouldn't say I've been getting sick of our undefined affiliation. I just keep wanting to know if and when things will change: Is he ever going to break up with Cassandra? Tell his sister about us? Get down on one knee with a big, fat chunk of ice and ask me to be the cream in his coffee until his cup runneth empty?

Uh, maybe not just yet. But about four seconds ago—after knocking me sideways with the news that he'll be home for his parents' twentieth-anniversary party next weekend—he *did* say something pretty extraordinary:

**JAS88:** I generally avoid sappy shit like anniversary parties, but what the hell? I figure I can look like a model son and see you at the same time.

Hello! Do you realize what this means? Jordan will use any excuse in the book to come see me! And in case you're not the sharpest needle in the haystack, that spells c-o-u-p-l-e. We may not have the label, but let's be honest, he's not exactly flying out to California to visit the old ball and chain at Stanford, now, is he? And that's because, deep down, he's secretly devoted to *me!* Now, if I could only get him to admit it. But first thing's first.

**JJ_Pearl:** So, how will this work? If I invite myself to stay over your house that night, won't Alona start getting suspicious?

**JAS88:** I think you overestimate my sister's mental capacity. Besides, I'm sure she'll end up inviting *you*. Alona hates these formal house parties as much as I do, and always insists on having her entourage there to entertain her.

**JJ_Pearl:** But I thought I'd be coming to entertain her big brother.

**JAS88:** I like the way you think.

**JJ_Pearl:** Hey, Jordan?

Here goes nothing . . .

**JJ_Pearl:** How do you feel about me?

**JAS88:** Horny.

Okay, I admit I'm smiling. Even if that wasn't exactly the response I had in mind.

**JAS88:** You mean you want a serious answer?

**JJ_Pearl:** Please.

**JAS88:** Okay, if you were just a little bit older . . . or I was just a little bit younger . . . or you weren't one of my sister's best friends . . . or I wasn't already with someone else . . .

**JJ_Pearl:** Someone you never see and don't love.

Okay, I know what you're thinking—that was risky. But it's like Alona said: They didn't name a fashion trend after me for nothing. So, uh ... why isn't Jordan responding?

**JJ_Pearl:** ?

*Oh, CG, you retarded little shit, why couldn't you just be content to play the game? Why do you* always *have to push people over the edge?*

**JAS88:** So, you think I love *you?*

Gulp. *Note to self: Find nearest bridge. Say a little prayer. Then jump.*

**JJ_Pearl:** No. I wasn't implying that at all.
**JAS88:** Too bad . . . because I do.

*Good evening. We once again interrupt your regular program for a special announcement regarding rebellious beauty CG Silverman. Inside sources reveal that we won't be bringing you any more special announcements about this teenager in love, because she has just officially died of shock.*

**JAS88:** You still there?
**JJ_Pearl:** Yeah.
**JJ_Pearl:** And I do, too.
**JAS88:** You do what? Love me?

Oh, God. What am I *doing?* Is this some kind of trap? No, wait, he said it first. Sort of. Hold on . . . Now, I'm confused.

**JAS88:** Listen, CG, I know all this may be confusing for you, but trust me, I have a lot of experience with relationships, and the stage we're in now really is the least complicated.
**JJ_Pearl:** You mean the sneaking-around stage where no one can find out about us and I don't even know what I am to you?
**JAS88:** You took me by surprise, CG. I never expected to feel this way. But it just wouldn't work out. At least, not now.
**JJ_Pearl:** Why not, though? I'm sure Alona would understand if you told her how you really feel about me. And if not, then *I'm* the one who should be running scared. I mean, who knows what kind of havoc your sister's wrath could wreak on my social life?

**JAS88:** LOL. Personally, I'm much more concerned with the wrath of the older generation There's a lot of pressure on Cassandra and me to be the perfect couple. Our parents expect us to get married right after college and have half a dozen babies crawling around before we even hit twenty-five.

**JJ_Pearl:** But you're not the perfect couple! You cheat on her and you're in love with me!

*Geez, say it, don't spray it.* Why do girls always do this? We play it cool as a cucumber in shades up until the moment Mr. Fabulous throws us a bone, and from there we do nothing but bleed our true colors—neediness, insecurity, desperation. I've seen it happen a million times. I just never thought I'd be a statistic.

**JAS88:** You're right, Cassandra and I are a mess. And I'll deal with it—eventually—in my own way. But that's between her and me. As for *you* and me, one of the things I love most about us is how relaxed things are. The sneaking around may seem weird to you, but it's a small price to pay for being together, don't you think?

**JJ_Pearl:** But how can we be "together" when you technically already have a girlfriend?

**JAS88:** What is it with women and labels? ☺

**JAS88:** Seriously, CG, you know what I was saying before about this stage being the least complicated? I meant the untitled stage. You've made me happier in two months than Cassandra has made me in the last two years

**JJ_Pearl:** Really??

**JAS88:** Yes, really. You mean so much more to me than a word.

**JJ_Pearl:** Really??

What am I, a freakin' Valley girl? Like, really? Totally? For sure?

**JAS88:** Maybe next weekend you'll give me a chance to express my gratitude, let me show you how much you mean to me. *Without* words.

Uh . . .

To be honest, I don't know how many more hookups we can endure without acknowledging the dirty elephant in the room—that is, the fact that if these makeout sessions were business meetings, he'd still be waiting to seal

the deal. Believe me, I'm not one of those naïve push-
over bimbettes who'd let just any guy sweet-talk her out
of her skivvies, but Jordan *did* say he loves me. And I love
him. And I *am* turning sixteen in two weeks. Juliet was
only thirteen. Just something to think about . . .

# twenty-four the truth about romeo

"May I interest you in another asparagus puff?" the bow-tied server asks, his tone about as sour and dry as my last bite of seasoned shrimp.

"No, thanks," I say. "One was definitely enough for me." Good lord, the food here tastes like ass. And Alona was right—her parents' parties *are* worse than school. The hired help can't even feign a pulse. And they're getting *paid* to be here.

Yes, everything went according to plan. Per my untitled someone's psychic prediction, Alona invited her entourage (read: Grace and me) to the Speltons' twentieth-anniversary soiree. But I'm telling you, if Jordan weren't here, I'd have bailed on this snoozer eons ago.

"Having fun?" And speaking of that sexalicious little devil!

"Tons," I say, turning to face him. *Hot damn.* I still can't get over how drop-dead he looks in that suit. No lie, the sizzle coming off Jordan's body right now would be enough to burn the roof off this yawnfest.

"Oh yeah, I can tell," he says with a friendly pinch of sarcasm. Smiling, he takes a step closer to me. "Have I mentioned how glad I am to see you?"

"No, but feel free."

"I've been counting down the minutes 'til we can be alone," Jordan whispers as he slips a covert hand around my waist.

"I didn't know you could count," I tease.

"Oh, you'd be surprised at all the special talents I've been hiding." He raises one eyebrow seductively. "Who do you think tied my shoes today?"

"Well, aren't you a big boy!"

He laughs, drawing me nearer. "So nice of you to notice."

I turn my head to see if anyone's watching, but Alona and Grace are way off in the distance, chatting it up with one of Sissy Spelton's spa acquaintances. So, I let myself fall into him a little, taking in the smell of his aftershave, his experience, his . . . *Jordanness.* Oh, for the sweet love of hormones, when is this wingding gonna finally be over?

"I wish I could kiss you right now," he says softly, his gentle lips grazing my ear.

"I wish you could, too. I can't wait for all these people to leave."

"Then, don't." *Uh, say what?* "Let's not wait."

I pull back to stare at him, confused. "I don't think your parents' guests would appreciate a halftime show."

Jordan shakes his head, smiling. "Sometimes I forget you're still learning."

"What's that supposed to mean?" I ask, my eyes drifting toward a pretty, middle-aged woman across the room who appears to be watching us.

"It means I like showing you the ropes . . corrupting your young, innocent mind." He reaches out to pinch my cheeks, but I smack his hand away playfully.

"I'm not as innocent as you think, buddy. You have no idea what goes on in this mind of mine."

"Oh yeah? Well, if you're really so mature, I dare you to meet me upstairs in five minutes. In my bed. Under the covers. Without that silly little dress on." *Um* .

"Did you say *dare?*"

He grins, nodding, his smoky blue eyes entreating me to go Nike and *Just do it*.

I look down at the floral frill job my mother made me wear to this root canal—let's just say rebel chic and catered galas at the Spelton crib don't mix—and helplessly shrug my shoulders. "This dress *is* pretty silly . . ." More importantly, what would Juliet do?

"So, is that a yes?" he asks, his face filling with hope.

"It's a—"

"Jordan!" a sweet-as-Splenda voice chirps from across the room. He quickly breaks away from me, like a criminal caught with his hand in the stolen cookie jar, and begins searching for the hidden intruder. "Jordan, honey! I've been trying to make my way over to you all evening!" The mysterious woman who seemed to be observing us a few moments ago is now running toward him with her arms outstretched. What's her *deal?* "Weren't you going to say hello to your future mother-in-law?"

*Oh, boy.* You'll have to forgive me. I think I just swallowed my tongue.

"Hey!" Jordan says warmly, giving her a big, giant octopus hug. "How *are* you?"

"Fine, fine," she answers, taking a step back to assess how much he's grown. You know how adults are, always marveling over what our parents must be feeding us and how fast time goes and how it seems like just yesterday when we were only *this* high . . . I don't normally mind the routine. Except when I'm watching the guy I love— the guy who's five lucky minutes away from possibly claiming my precious maidenhood—get doted on by his *girlfriend's* mother. "Oh, I wish Cassandra were here to see how handsome you look." Catch my drift?

"Well, I called her just before everyone got here." *Say WHAT?* "She made me promise to e-mail her tons of pictures later, so don't worry—Cass will get to see how well I cleaned up for this party." *Cass?* Make me barf.

"Aw," she gushes, oozing with sentimental stickiness. "You two are so sweet together." *No they're not! Can't you see he's only with her because he feels like he has to be, that all this pressure you're putting on him is keeping us apart?* "Hey, listen," she says, huddling close as if she's about to divulge a government secret, "I want you to know Cass told me all about Cape Cod, and I think it's an extraordinary idea. Dexter and I never have time to use the cottage anyway, so why shouldn't you two enjoy it?" She lets out a long, wistful sigh. "A whole summer on the Cape. If only I were nineteen again...You and Cass are going to have a blast."

Okay, say *DOUBLE WHAT?* I thought Jordan didn't love this girl, and now I find out he not only called her just moments before our big date, but that he's planning to spend the entire summer playing house with her in friggin' New England?

"Who knows," Mama Cass continues, raising a jesting brow, "maybe she'll even come back with a little something shiny on that left hand of hers." She giggles, wrapping her arms around Jordan in another vomit-inducing display of "motherly" affection. "You know I'm only teasing. The amethyst promise ring you gave her on Easter was enough to keep Cass happy for at least a couple more years."

Oh no. Tell me I did not just hear that. Jordan gave Cassandra a *promise ring?* Just one day after we fooled around in that hotel room? I didn't even know he saw her that weekend.

Jordan smiles bashfully.

"Oh, come on," Mama Cass says, tousling his hair. "You thought I wouldn't find out about the ring? Please. You know my daughter can't keep a secret to save her own life! I'm acutely aware of all your future plans, including the one to make me a grandmother of six by the time you're both twenty-five." Wait, I thought those were their *parents'* plans, not Jordan and Cassandra's. She laughs, turning to me. "Are all young people in such a rush to grow up these days?"

I shrug, my eyes brimming with tears because I know the answer is yes. To think I ever considered losing my virginity to such a manipulative snake in the grass. I don't know who I should be more afraid of—him or myself for having such atrociously terrible judgment.

"How rude of me," Mama Cass confesses, turning back to Jordan. "I haven't even introduced myself to your friend. Hi," she says, facing me again, "I'm Ruby Britman."

And I'm *puking*. I mean, whose name is ever honestly *Ruby?* Leave it to Jordan's future mother-in-law to claim that glorified distinction. Actually, she really is a stunning woman . . . the *bitch*. As I take a moment to absorb her red-carpet features—creamy, café au lait skin; rich, shimmery brown eyes; silky, shampoo-spokesmodel hair; a smile that could blind the dead—I can only hope "Cass" takes after her father. Then again, with my luck, Papa Cass is probably gorgeous, too. Just like Jordan. Who was I to think I could ever have a place inside his glamorous world? Let's face it, in my untitled romance with my untitled Romeo, I'm always gonna be the girl he meets behind closed doors for a quickie, never the one who gets the promise ring. So, if I know this, what am I even sticking around for?

"It's nice to meet you, Ruby," I say, smiling weakly. "If you'll both excuse me . . . I think I may have eaten some bad shrimp."

\* \* \*

Trying not to cry . . . trying not to cry . . . I have no idea how long I've been locked inside this bathroom, but I can tell you I've never in my life seen so many fancy soaps shaped like Marshmallow Peeps. I wonder what would happen if I decided to just go ahead and eat one. Maybe I'd die and all these retarded little chickie soaps would be forced to hold a toilet-side funeral in my honor. And then I'd never have to go back out to that party and deal with the scheming con artist who broke my heart.

*Knock knock.*

"Somebody's in here!" I call out. That must be the third person who's banged on the door since I set up shop.

*Knock knock.* And apparently, *this* jerkmeister can't even comprehend simple English.

"I *said,* somebody's in here," I bark, giving the doorknob an angry twist, only to come face to face with America's Next Top Con Man. He takes a quick step into the bathroom, closing the door behind him. "What do you think you're doing?" I ask.

"We need to talk."

"About what?" I demand, folding my arms. "The pre-engagement ring you bought your girlfriend or the summer home you'll be sharing on the Cape?"

Jordan frowns sadly, waiting for me to finish.

"You told me you were only with her because of everyone else's expectations, but that's not true, is it?" I ask. "It's not your parents or the Britmans that are forcing you to get married and give them all those grandkids by the time you're twenty-five. It's what *you* want."

"It's what *she* wants!" he snaps.

"And you care what she wants because …?" I hold my hands out in front of me, stumped for logic.

Jordan shrugs, staring down at the floor. "You don't know her, okay? Cassandra's a good person."

"That's *it?*" I ask, completely dumbstruck. "She's 'a good person'?"

He nods, looking up at me blankly as if only an illiterate baboon who just fell off the turnip truck by way of the banana boat could ever be confused by such a hollow explanation.

"Jordan, *Bono* is a good person," I point out. "Does this mean you're also planning to shower *him* with sentimental jewelry and romantic summers on the shore?"

"I'm not in love with Bono."

*What?* Did he just say what I think he said? Warning: You may want to put the kiddies to bed. Because this is where I mother-humping lose it.

"You fucking liar!" I scream. "You told me you didn't love her! You said *I* was the one you cared about, remember? Or was that all just part of some bullshit plan to get in my pants?"

"Ssh!" he commands, grabbing hold of my wrists.

Oh, did I mention I was beating the crap out of him? "CG, calm down. You've gotta stop hitting me."

"Don't change the subject!" I yell. Besides, what are a few bruises compared with my heart, my happiness, my sweet little ever-after?

"All right, look," he says, "it was never my intention to lie to you. I just didn't think you'd understand."

"Understand what?" I snarl, wriggling like an epileptic earthworm in his grip. *Not* wanting Jordan's hands on me—now, *that's* a switch. "That you're a two-faced son of a bitch?"

"That it *is* possible to have feelings for more than one person."

"I guess I know what that's like," I reluctantly admit. "So, why didn't you just tell me the truth?"

"Because I'm confused," he says, letting go of me. "I don't even know what 'the truth' is anymore. I thought Cass and I would be together forever—until we went our separate ways to college and I realized I just wasn't cut out for the whole commitment thing. At least, not at this point in my life. But none of the girls I fooled around with ever meant anything to me . . . until you. And now I can't get you off my mind."

"And the ring?" I ask, refusing to let him sweet-talk his way past my line of fire.

"Oh, that. Well . . ." he fumbles. "I gave it to her because I knew she was expecting it. And I do want to marry her *someday* . . . I think." He takes my face in his hands, eagerly cupping my chin. "But I don't want to lose what you and I have right now. You make me feel so good, CG." He smiles suggestively. "And I know you can make me feel even better." Okay, am I challenged or did this guy just ask me to be his whore?

"So, let me see if I've got this straight," I say, removing his paws from my face. "You want to keep seeing us both?"

He nods, his eyes brightening.

"Only, when you picture your real life—the part that comes after your days as a selfish bastard—you picture it with *her*. Married and with kids. And in the meantime, I sleep with you whenever you're home, fatten your ego, act as the all-around perfect back-seat bimbo. Is that what you had in mind?"

"CG, you're overthinking this."

"Well, one of us has to. Have you ever thought of what you're doing to me at all? Of what you're doing to *her?* I mean, how devastated would Cassandra be to learn that her 'perfect boyfriend' has been screwing everything that moves since the day she let him out of her sight?"

"There's no such thing as the perfect boyfriend," he says regretfully. "We're all pigs, some just filthier than others."

"I don't think that's true."

Jordan shakes his head. "Then you're more naïve than I thought."

"Maybe. But I'll stay that way for as long as I can if it means believing nice guys still exist. Even though a lying dirtbag like you could never be one of them. Now, let me out of this bathroom."

"Or what?" he asks, blocking my exit.

"Or at the count of five, I start screaming for Mrs. Britman. I'm sure our good pal Ruby would be just fascinated to know what we've been talking about in here. One . . . two . . ."

I'm not sure if this is how Juliet would've handled things, but my little threat does force Jordan to back away from the door. And besides, Juliet's dead anyway, so what the hell was I modeling myself after her for?

On my way out of the bathroom, my former prince stares at me coldly. "I can't believe I wasted my time on an immature brat like you. You know, you're not even that hot."

Charming, huh? Ignoring his anger—and the salty, gaping wound in my heart—I brush past him with my head held high, bursting into tears just moments after my feet hit the hallway.

★ ★ ★

"Hey, CG, is your stomach feeling any better?" Alona asks, tiptoeing over to the bed with a mug of steaming hot tea. "My mom made this for you. She feels really bad about the shrimp."

Okay, rewind. About an hour ago, when Alona caught me crying in the hallway after my big blowout with the king of the prickwads, I figured, why not blame the little guys again? I mean, the bad shrimp excuse worked when I met Ruby Britman, and if I've learned anything about telling lies, it's that it's always best to stick to the same one. Actually, it's probably better to just tell the truth, but unfortunately, I never seem to have that option.

"Oh, tell her I said thanks. I'll be down in a bit."

"Take your time," Alona says, setting the mug down on her nightstand. "I need a few minutes up here, anyway. I want to change into my second outfit."

"You mean you bought two outfits for this party?" I ask. Who is she, JLo?

"Three," she remarks casually, completely failing to recognize the absurdity of needing to perform two wardrobe changes in order to stand and eat crappy food in her own living room.

"You know, I've never met anyone like you, Lonnie."

"I'll take that as a compliment," she says, flashing one of her signature centerfold smiles. "Oh, by the way, the weirdest thing: Grace and I were both trapped in this torturous conversation downstairs with my cousin Mitzie, and all of a sudden I turn around and Grace has *totally* disappeared."

"As in vanished?"

"Without a trace," Alona confirms. "I haven't seen her in, like, a half hour. I've looked everywhere."

"Maybe she was abducted by a gang of angry asparagus puffs," I say, rising from the bed.

Alona giggles as I begin making my way toward the door. "Going somewhere?" she asks.

"Yeah, I need to send a few more of those shrimp back to sea before we head downstairs."

"Um, *ew.* CG, that was totally TMI."

"Sorry." Truth is, I think it's time to go survey the damage my little hissy fit wreaked on my appearance. I mean, I may not be out to impress old What's His Name anymore, but I've gotta draw the line somewhere. Like, say, just short of a blotchy, hive-stricken face dripping in mascara and snot. I could never let that ass clown think he got the best of me.

"Hey, CG," Alona calls as I open the door to leave. Her gaze has suddenly turned pensive, almost sentimental.

"What is it?"

"I've never met anyone like you, either."

Am I on some kind of mind-altering hallucinogenic, or did this girl and I just have a Hallmark moment? If so, I've gotta admit I'm sort of touched. She may still be as shallow as a tub full of air, but in her own special way, Alona really does care about me, which is a hell of a lot more than I can say for her brother.

As I head toward the bathroom, the door at the other end of the hall swings open—the door leading straight to Jordan's dungeon. *Crap.* Ignoring him amid a crowded room of middle-aged farts I could've handled—I was all set to go downstairs and be the ultimate megabitch—but a direct, one-on-one face-off right here in the hallway? What in the name of spit am I gonna say when he walks out?

*"Grace?"* That's right, you heard me. Look who I caught sneaking away from the vulture's nest.

"Ssh!" she cautions, waving me backwards as she fumbles with the buttons on her blouse. Geez. Romeo didn't waste any time, did he? I guess that solves the mystery of the vanishing party guest. I wonder what she's planning to tell Alona. "Just get out of here, CG, all right?" Oh my God, she's *crying.*

"Wait, what happened in there? What did he do to you?"

"Nothing," she says, using her sleeve to dry her eyes. "It was nothing."

"Hey, you two wanna keep it down?"

Well, if it isn't the man of the hour, standing before us in nothing but a white cotton bedsheet. And fine, I admit he's still hotter than brimstone. But you know, aside from the whole Calvin Klein underwear model thing, he's really nothing more than a spoiled little rich boy who can't keep his rooster in his pants.

"Jordan, go to your room!" I shout.

"Anything else, Mom?" he asks, an arrogant smirk playing upon his pouty lips.

"Yeah, drop dead, you scumsucking son of a bitch." Damn, how good did *that* feel? (You might want to hold your applause until the end of the show.)

★ ★ ★

"You shouldn't have done that," Grace reprimands, her eyes wide with warning. I've just led her into the john, where I'm hoping she'll feel safe enough to tell me what happened. "Nobody talks to him that way."

"He'll live." *Unfortunately.*

She gazes down at the gold ceramic tiles on the bathroom floor—the same tiles Schmucky and I got cozy on just a couple of weeks ago—and begins tracing a pattern with her shoe. She's stalling.

"Well?" I say finally. "Are you gonna tell me what happened?"

Grace looks up at me, shaking her head. "You wouldn't understand." The tears are back again—in full force. "I'm in love with him, okay?"

*"In love?"* I ask, totally mystified. "But how is that possible? You guys don't even talk."

"We used to—all the time—until *you* came along."

"You mean . . ." How do I phrase this gently? "Back when you were stalking him?" I shrug helplessly. "Well, you know, that's what *he* called it."

"I remember," she says icily. "You told me. And *that's* when we stopped talking. Because that's when I knew for sure."

"Knew what?"

"That I'd been replaced." She crosses over to the bathtub and sits. "CG, in case you haven't noticed, the day God was handing out common sense, Sammie and Alona were in the back of the line snorting Pixie Sticks. They may not have suspected something was going on between you and Jordan, but I always did, starting with that first night when we dared you to go into his room.

Did you really expect me to believe you were in there all that time 'just talking'?"

"I guess not," I say softly. I mean, what's the point of pretending anymore? We've both got enough dirt on each other to bury this whole house in shit, and besides, I've grown tired of lying. The price just keeps getting higher, and in case I haven't mentioned it, I'm not exactly a wealthy woman.

"He started blowing me off almost immediately after your little dare—I knew I no longer had his attention. I didn't hate you because I was jealous of your Internet fling with Mr. F. Or because you were smarter or more rebellious or Alona's newest pet. I hated you for stealing Jordan away from me."

"And I hated *you* for ever being with him in the first place. But don't you see? He's not ours to hate. He already *has* a girlfriend."

"Yeah," Grace says, nodding bitterly. "A virgin who goes to school three thousand miles away and won't sleep with him for at least another two years until they're married."

Oh.

"I had no idea Cassandra was a virgin." I can tell by the way she's looking at me that Grace thinks I'm dumber than dog shit. On second thought, make that dog dingleberries.

"Why *else* would he have kept me around all this time?" she asks bluntly. "Men have needs, CG. Especially men whose Bible-thumping girlfriends refuse to give it up."

"But wait a second. I'm confused. Jordan told me you guys only got together once. He made it seem like nothing." Um . . . probably *not* the smartest thing to say. Grace begins to sob like a wounded seal as I make my way over to the tub and sit, cautiously wrapping my arms around her. "I'm sorry I believed him," I tell her. "I guess it was just the first of many lies."

"I tried to warn you," she cries. "We may have had our differences, but I wanted to protect you from him. He treats women like random scraps of garbage, CG, without any feeling or conscience about it at all."

"Well, then, why do you put up with him?" I ask. "I mean, how can you say you're in love with someone who has absolutely no respect for you whatsoever?"

She pulls away from me, taking a deep breath. "Remember that night up on the balcony, the camp counselor I told you about?"

I nod. "Yeah, so?"

"I never went to overnight camp. Jordan's the older guy who showed me attention when no one else would. He's the one I've spent the last two years pining after."

*"Two years?"* I echo. "So, the first time you had sex, you were only thirteen?"

"I had just turned fourteen," she clarifies. As if the distinction makes this whole thing any less disturbing. "It was right after middle school graduation. My mom was seeing this guy who owned a summer share in the Hamptons, and I'd gone away with them for the week. Meanwhile, the Speltons have a place up there, which Jordan and a bunch of his senior buddies had turned into party central for the class of '06. Let's just say I found the party and Jordan found me." Using the back of her hand, Grace wipes her eyes. Sniffs. "He told me about his girlfriend the night I met him, said she was kind of a drag and hadn't even felt like making the trip to celebrate their grand achievement. But that worked out well. We spent the whole week together, side-by-side inseparable, falling in love—or so I thought—and then he just sort of dropped me . . . Until I showed up on his doorstep a few months later—as his sister's new best friend—to remind him of just how much fun I could be."

"So, wait a second," I say as the shock surges through me like a mind-numbing case of the runs. "Are you telling me you sought Alona out on purpose just because you were in love with her brother?" *Isn't that a little, oh, I don't know . . . PSYCHOTIC of you?*

"Well, it's no different from seeking her out because she's popular. Or because our fathers work together and I'm trying to get closer to Daddy, which is what she admittedly did with you." Okay, Nutbar does have a point there, but just because something's legal doesn't mean it's kosher. I know that much from Hebrew school. "Besides, it's not as if I haven't grown to love her independently of her family tree. And if I ever had to choose between them, God knows I'd choose Alona. Jordan's no good for me. Hell, CG, at least give me credit for being wise enough to know that."

"But if you know it, what were you just doing in his room?"

"Saying goodbye."

"With your clothes off?"

She smiles weakly. "It didn't start out that way. He sent me a text message saying we had to talk. I figured he was finally going to tell me about you, that he'd say things were *finito* and he wanted me back. I mean, why else would he be bothering with me after all this time unless your little fling had gone belly up? But instead of feeling happy, I was ready to tell him *we* were finished, too, that I was tired of living my life for a guy who walks all over me. But I never got the chance—he started kissing me the second I walked in the door. It was like we picked up right where we'd left off, but it wasn't long before that same old voice started ringing in my head, the one that always said: *He's only with you because he can't have her.* But this time, instead of Snow White Cassandra, it was *you* he wanted to make love to when he decided to settle for a cheap and easy ride with his favorite doormat. I just couldn't do it—I knew I couldn't be his second choice anymore. So I jumped up off the bed, told him it wasn't going to happen. And I left."

"And that's when you bumped into me."

She nods, straightening up. "I'm sorry I'm such a mess. I haven't been *this* bad since he dropped me on my ass two years ago. Oddly enough, it was that creepazoid neighbor of yours, Glory Finkle*freak,* who was there to witness the wreck. She's the only other person who's ever seen me break down over him."

"Wait, *Glory* knows about this?" Why didn't she ever say anything to me? Like... I don't know... any of the seven hundred *gazillion* times I mentioned Jordan was my boyfriend? Come to think of it, she did sort of look like she'd choked on an atomic warhead the first time I told her about us. But I thought that was a good thing.

"Well, I needed *someone* to talk to and we *were* best friends." Oh, so now she admits it?

"Well, if that's true, why do you hate her so much?"

"Because she's a freaking narc, that's why! You know, it wasn't even two hours after I told her about my romantic week with Jordan in the Hamptons that my mom knew every last detail. Of course, my mother couldn't have cared less," Grace continues cavalierly, "but that's

hardly the point. The point is, that girl has a mouth bigger than Texas and can't be trusted to save her own life.
I'm surprised she hasn't told the whole school all about
me and my sexcapades by now. Come to think of it,"
she says, her wheels clearly turning as she rises from the
edge of the tub, "I'm willing to bet the house it was *Glory*
who's responsible for that little smear job on MySpace.
You heard her threaten me on the phone that night.
And let's face it, Sammie's not exactly smart enough to
pull off such a sophisticated stunt."

"She's a lot smarter than you give her credit for,"
I point out. Granted, Grace may be one wounded flower,
but her bruises don't give her the right to sit here and
fire cheap shots at two of the nicest girls I've ever known.
It's time to do the right thing (if I can still remember
what that is). "And Glory was just trying to look out
for you," I continue. "That doesn't make her a narc. It
makes her a friend. A damn good one, if you ask me."

Grace crinkles her brow. "I thought she was just your
neighbor."

"And I thought *you* were still a virgin."

"Ha ha," she says, sneering. "Just watch what you
tell her."

"Oh, come on. You're not upset with Glory for letting your mom know what was going on right under
her very nose that week in the Hamptons. You're upset

because your mom didn't care. You're embarrassed because you can't stand for anyone to see how vulnerable you really are, but Glory's not the one who let you down. Jordan let you down. Your mother, with all her boyfriends; your father and his second family—*they* let you down. You take things out on the wrong people, Grace. I've watched you lash out at me, Sammie, Glory, and the world when maybe the person you're most angry at is yourself."

"Who are you, my priest?" she asks coldly. "Besides, despite your glittering analysis of my inner psyche, you still can't prove old Dorkelfuss didn't do that MySpace thing."

"Yes, I can." Here goes nothing . . . Make that *the right thing.* "Because I did it."

"You WHAT?"

Have you ever seen one of those movies where the good guy turns into a vicious werewolf or something, like totally out of the blue? Well, she's not a guy, and the jury's still out on how *good* she is, but I'm pretty sure Grace just sprouted whiskers and fangs. That is, *before* she took me down. I believe the boxing term for this is TKO. I can't believe she actually hit me.

"You *bitch!*" she yells over my crumpled physique, which has landed plunk in the center of the freezing marble bathtub. Fortunately, the warm blood spilling from my nasal passages is enough to fend off the hypothermia. "How could you do that to me?"

Suddenly, the door bursts open. Clutching my nose, I try to focus, but all I can make out is a tall, dark ball of fuzz.

"I heard a thud," the Fuzzball says. Perfect—it's *Jordan*. And I thought things couldn't possibly get any worse. "What happened? Holy shit, is she okay?"

"She's fine," Grace says quickly. "She just fell, that's all."

"Looks like the tub made quite an impression on you," Jordan observes. Is he making *jokes*? At a time like *this*?

I clear my throat. "Could, uh, someone help me up, please?"

A hazy white image flitters into the room. Please tell me it's an angel, here to rescue me from this horrifying shitstorm.

"Grace, there you are!" Alona's effervescent voice is unmistakable. What was I just saying about a shitstorm? This is more like a diarrhea hurricane. And with our ringleader here, it looks like all the mourners have arrived just in time to watch me bury myself alive. "I've been looking all over for—omigod, what happened to CG?"

"She fell," Jordan and Grace answer simultaneously, almost as if on cue. *Uh, the harmony was perfect, you guys, but next time, sing it with feeling.*

"And you two were just gonna leave her lying there?" Alona asks.

My vision begins to sharpen as my "angel of mercy" lifts me from the tub, handing me a wad of tissues for the sniffer. Everyone's staring at me as if I'm some kind of freak show. Hey, I didn't punch *myself* in the nose.

"You took a pretty nasty spill," Alona says. "Was the floor wet or something? How exactly did you fall?"

"I didn't." *This is it . . .* "Grace hit me." Like I said before, I'm tired of lying. Look at where it's gotten me.

"You *hit* her?" Alona asks, turning to She-Wolf. Grace looks away, clearly ashamed.

"It's okay, I deserved it."

"You did?" Jordan asks, appearing nothing short of innocent in his tailored three-piece suit. *Back to being the model boy scout, I see.* Well, he may be as fake as a politician's promise, but I'm not. Not anymore.

"I haven't been honest with you," I tell Alona. "About anything. I was the one who posted that blog a couple of weeks ago telling the entire MySpace community Grace was a dope-addicted nympho."

"That was *you?*" Jordan asks, plainly amused.

Ignoring him, I proceed to clear the rest of my cluttered conscience. "I was angry at her for setting up that crank call . . . Glory Finklefuss is one of my closest friends—or at least, she used to be."

"Used to be?" Alona repeats skeptically, folding her arms across her chest.

I shrug. "It seems she has a low threshold for liars."

"Meaning?" Alona demands, growing impatient.

"I'm not a rebel, okay? If anything, I'm the biggest scaredy cat I know, definitely not some kind of daredevil wild child. And all that talk about living dangerously . . . I've never even *tasted* a sip of alcohol, let alone had a drinking problem, which, for the record, makes me the *worst* possible role model for recovering teenage alcoholics this world has ever seen. I have no friggin' idea what I'm even talking about at those meetings!"

"Are you *kidding* me?" Alona asks. "Why on earth would you make something like that up?"

"Because I got carried away. Just like I got carried away trying to impress everyone the night I told you about my ex. Alex was my best friend who I wrote off because I was in such a rush to move up here and prove I could actually be somebody. I had a crush on him, but we never dated, and we certainly never had sex."

"What?" Grace barks. "You mean, you're still a *virgin?*"

"Boring, but true," I say. "It was just so much easier to lie—to create this intriguing character you'd all fall in love with—than to show any of you who I really was."

"So, who *are* you?" Alona asks, her chilly tone throbbing with disapproval. For the first time, I'm getting a chance to see Her Majesty the way everybody else does—as the snooty, untouchable ice princess who never lets anyone get too close. Only the ice princess did thaw a little for me. I just blew it big time, that's all.

"I'd say I'm a girl who cracks her gum out of habit—not to torment homeroom teachers. A girl who chooses her clothes because they're comfortable and won't break the bank—not because she's the antichrist of fashion. A girl who never went to second with Bill Fenowitz."

"Just stop," Alona says, holding her hands out in front of her. "This is getting way too weird." Everyone's quiet for a few seconds while Queenie stares down at the floor, contemplating my fate. "Are you saying you lied because you were afraid we wouldn't accept you?" she asks finally.

"I guess that's a fair assessment."

"You know," she says, cocking her pretty blond head to one side, "Dr. Phil has a saying that we create what we fear." *Not a good time to roll your eyes, CG.* "Because you were so afraid of losing me, you went to these tremendous extremes to avoid it, and in the end, wound up accomplishing your worst nightmare."

Hold on a sec. Wouldn't my *worst nightmare* be more along the lines of, say, death, dismemberment, or, I don't know, maybe nuclear destruction? I mean, I always knew Alona's priorities were a little screwy, but does she honestly think the most catastrophic tragedy I could possibly fathom would be the evaporation of our superficial friendship?

"You know something," I say, heading for the door. I am so outta here. The three of them deserve each other. "I'll be okay if you will."

★ ★ ★

All right, I just made an important discovery—aside from the fact that next time I decide to hightail it home from a party without transportation, I should first check to make sure it's not storming outside—and that two minus two really does equal zero. Without Grace and Alona, it's gonna be Solo City back at school. What am I gonna do? Who will I talk to? Who will I *eat lunch* with? I mean, I can deal with unpopular, but a social pariah? *God, if you have any love for me at all, you'll send a fat, juicy bolt of lightning my way, finish me off before Monday morning.*

Nothing.

*Still waiting . . .*

Well, would ya look at that? Even the big man upstairs has me on his shit list. Let that be a lesson to all you kiddies out there: Not even God likes a poser. You know, Jordan and I weren't really all that different. Maybe that's why I couldn't rat him out to Alona. It would be like that whole pot-calling-the-kettle-black thing, or in this case, the fraud calling the liar phony. Besides, Alona and I were only friends for three months. Jordan's gonna be her big brother forever. I guess I just didn't have the heart to ruin his image. In time, I'm sure he'll do that all on his own.

The sky changes from dark to darker as a dull rumbling roars in the distance. Okay, we've got thunder. Now, let there be lightning. Between two navy storm-clouds, a jagged bolt of energy surges through the atmosphere. Far, far away from me.

"Oh, come on!" I yell. "Are you really so cheap you can't spare a rod? Or maybe you just hate me too much to let me off easy—you'd rather I suffer for my sins. Is that it? Well, let me tell you something, *Mister* Almighty. You have one seriously disturbed view of humanity if you think you can just go around shedding all your sacred mercy on murderers, rapists, and every other sick, twisted fruit that's managed to shake itself loose from the Scruples Tree, and yet when it comes to me—a virtual saint by comparison—all you can do is turn the other cheek. And I'm not even asking for forgiveness! I *want* to be put out of my misery! How is it you can give all these brutal savages the compassion *they* pray for, but little CG Silverman tells a few measly lies to a bunch of random high school kids and you completely shut down on her? What's wrong with this picture? Shed a little mercy on *me!*"

"Excuse me, miss? Do you need a ride?"

*God? Is that you?* Um ... On second thought, unless God is an obese, balding Chinese man in a red pickup truck, staring at me like I'm crazy, I'm gonna venture to guess this isn't divine intervention. Wait a minute—I *am* crazy. I've just turned into one of those screaming hystericals who stands outside on the street corner throwing tantrums at God.

"Miss? You do realize you're drenched? Lucky for you, I've got a nice warm blanket in my trunk. Why don't you hop in and let me dry you off?"

I don't answer him, because I'm already running. And even though he isn't following me, I keep on running—through the thunder, the rain, the lightning, and my tears until I've finally made it home sweet home.

# twenty-five paying double

To those who say life at the top is lonely, may I kindly suggest life at the bottom? Because trust me, you haven't met loneliness until you've spent the entire week eating lunch in a bathroom stall amid the sounds—not to mention smells—of disgruntled bowels. But solitary confinement, even the stinky kind, is still superior to the public humiliation I'd suffer if I dined in the cafeteria. The world already knows I went from Four Top to friendless in a matter of a weekend. Why flaunt my leper's status by letting the whole school watch me eat alone? If anyone's really that hungry for a show, they can come see me chow down every afternoon at one o'clock in the third-floor ladies' john, second stall from the window. Be there or be square.

Actually, the sad thing is, I've gotten kind of used to it. I don't talk to anybody and nobody talks to me. I guess everyone's just playing it safe, figuring I must've done *something* totally horrendous to end up on Alona's bad side and that associating with me could have devastating effects on their social karma. I will give Her Majesty credit for one thing, though. She could've totally sold me out and she didn't. As far as I'm aware, no one knows what went wrong, which means I may be a certified loser, but at least I'm not walking around with a giant KICK ME sign taped to my hoodie. Which reminds me: Rebel chic can officially go down as the shortest-lived fashion trend ever. As for DAAG, I heard the group disbanded due to lack of organization—like loss of its bogus alcoholic president, maybe—but no one's pointed any fingers at me, so again, I give kudos to the queen bee of Beaubridge for not stinging as hard as she could have.

To tell you the truth, despite my brave exterior, my new social status (or lack thereof) is actually a whole lot worse than I'm making it seem. I guess I've just been trying not to wallow. Because if I let myself dwell too much on how I got here—on the supreme stupidity that led me to deceive the people I cared most about, not to mention the rest of the planet—I'd never make it off the shitter. I mean, Alona may be as fake as the silicone job on Hugh Hefner's latest teen bimbo, but, hey, at least she's up-front about it. I, on the other hand, have been the worst kind of fraud—the kind nobody can trust. To think I literally went from the top of the world to the toilet bowl—without so much as a shred of decency or common sense to even once slap me in the chubby, freckled face and say, "What the donkey dick are you *doing?*"—is almost beyond comprehension. If I let myself think about it for too long, trapped with my conscience amid those dreary, isolating walls of my bathroom prison, the only thing I can do is cry. And then my thoughts turn to Alex.

Alex Kerper was the best friend I ever had, and I cut him out of my life. When I think about him, when I remember the magical fluidity of our friendship and how easy it was to just "be" together—to just be *myself*— I ache for the past so bad I can feel it in my toenails. A few nights ago, I finally broke down and did something about it.

Dialing his number felt strange. Talking every night used to be as automatic as my morning tinkle. But now, who knew if he'd even recognize my voice?

"Hello?"

I definitely recognized his. Soaking in the familiar, homegrown tone of his softspoken greeting, I completely lost my composure and began sobbing like a newborn baby.

"Hello?" he repeated. "Who is this?"

"Alex," I stammered. "It's me."

*"Cindy?"*

Oh yeah. One other small thing I forgot to mention. My name isn't really CG. I mean, I guess it *could* be—same way Alona Jayne Spelton's name could be AJ—but for the first fifteen years and nine months of my life, the world merely knew me as Cindy. The CG thing was all part of my master plan to reinvent myself when I first came to Beaubridge. I figured if Madonna and Britney could keep doing it, why not me?

"What's the matter?" Alex asked. "Is something wrong?"

"I just . . ." I trailed off, hoping to catch my breath. "I miss you. And I really need a friend."

As it turns out, that was all that needed to be said. In the end, my old buddy Alex was still willing to be there for me, the same way he'd always been—every day of my life since the seventh grade (give or take a few regrettable months). Knowing I can still turn to him sort of makes having lunch on the dumper a little bit easier to take.

But enough about school. Why? Because it's Friday, and I'm leaving my penance behind for the next forty-eight hours to focus on the parts of my life that don't absolutely suck to high hell. Like the weather, for instance. I decided to ditch the bus and walk home this afternoon so I could spend a little quality time communing with

Mother Nature, the only bitch in this town who can stand to be around me for more than five minutes.

Spring may have dragged its frilly little heels getting here, but I tell you, southeastern Pennsylvania is definitely in full bloom today. And it was well worth the wait. The sun is shining, birds are chirping, and the air smells like fresh-cut grass and girls about to turn sixteen. That's right, you heard me—tomorrow's my freakin' *birthday!* Which means, pretty soon I'll be able to bust this burg and all its catty melodrama and peddle my ass back to Philly any time I want. Not that I'd be going to visit anyone *in particular* . . . Okay, you beat it out of me: Alex and I are so incredibly back on track—talking on the phone every day for hours, laughing at all our old inside jokes—that I honestly can't remember how I ever functioned without him. Come to think of it, I *didn't*. I lied, scammed, lost every friend I had, and failed to actually tell *anyone* my real name. Alex now knows all about my downward descent into No Man's Land—including how I almost slept with Jordan—and says the biggest mistake he ever made was asking me to be his girlfriend.

"Gee, thanks," I said when he laid *that* confidence booster on me.

"No, I just mean if I hadn't made things so awkward, you wouldn't have waited such a long time to tell me all this. Maybe I could've helped." Okay, if this boy were any sweeter, I'd be in sugar shock.

"It wasn't you," I insisted. "It was me. After three and a half years as your little tagalong tomboy sidekick, I was ready to move up here and be somebody special. For once. Without anything, or anyone, holding me back."

"Makes sense," he conceded. "But I always thought I was *your* sidekick, which was very emasculating, really. My shrink says our friendship played a pivotal role in my gender identity crisis. So, just remember when I have that sex-change operation—it was all your fault." Sweet *and* hilarious. God, I really did miss him. "Anyway, at this point, I guess it's time for Plan B."

"Plan B?" *You mean skip the long-distance romance and just move in together?* All right, so my secret's out: I never stopped loving him. The question is, what's *he* gonna do about it now?

"Hey, the cool crowd thing may have ended in disaster, but that doesn't mean my little tagalong tomboy deserves to be eating lunch every day on the shitter. Don't worry, we'll come up with something. And if all else fails, there's always the option of faking your own death. Who knows? Just because the kids at school aren't willing to touch *CG* with a ten-foot baton doesn't mean they wouldn't graciously welcome her grieving identical cousin *Cindy* into their social stratosphere.

Happened just the other day on one of my mother's soaps. And we all know how credible *those* things are, right?"

"Right," I said dismally, realizing that whatever had motivated Alex to ask me out before I moved must've officially died with my popularity. Like he said, it was the worst mistake he ever made. Oh well. At least I have my best friend back. And if he doesn't send me a mushy e-card dripping in sentimental drool for my big one-six, I'll kill him.

★ ★ ★

"Mom!" I call out cheerfully as I burst through the front door. "I'm home!"

"I'm in the kitchen," she answers. "With your *father*."

Say who? My dad's never here when I get home from school. Something has to be wrong ... He's dying. No, *she's* dying and he came home early to help her break the news to me. Or they could *both* have devastating news to break ... Oh, holy shit stains—they're getting a divorce! I knew this whole Waltons thing was too perfect to last.

*Relax,* I tell myself, *maybe he just got laid off or something. ... As if that's supposed to be GOOD NEWS?? What kind of daughter are you?*

Okay, now I'm fighting with the voices in my head. Is that better or worse than fighting with God in the rain?

Ooh, wait, I know! My father's noticed what a funky mood I've been in on account of losing every friend I ever had in Beaubridge (and, consequently, becoming the town reject), so he came home early hoping to lift my spirits with a prebirthday bash at some really great restaurant in the city—you know, to help me kick-start the year in style? That's *it!* An impromptu sweet sixteen celebration dinner with the folks. I'll try to act surprised.

"Hey!" I say, entering the kitchen. I toss my bookbag onto the counter and bend down to give them each a hug. Okay, not to diss my parents here, but I've received warmer receptions from mannequins at the mall. "What's going on?"

"I don't know," my mother responds numbly. "Why don't you tell us?"

"What do you mean?" I ask, searching their cold, stony faces for some sign of a clue. My father won't even look at me, which, in itself, is a very bad sign.

"Have a seat," my mom says, nodding toward one of the oak-finish chairs that surround our simple wooden table. I can see that it has already been pulled out for me. Again, not exactly a winning indication. She watches me assume my place, then clears her throat for what seems like a small eternity. "I ran into Mrs. Finklefuss at the Farmer's Market this morning," she says finally, reaching for the full glass of water that sits in front of her. "She said she'd been talking to one of the PTA moms at your school." *Um . . . and this has* what *to do with me?* My mom takes an extended sip of her drink, and I notice that my father also has one. They must be planning one hell of a lecture. Oh, for the sake of daughters everywhere, *what* did I do? My mother sets her glass down, looking at me strangely. "Since when are you an alcoholic?" Oh, *that.*

"Uh . . ." What was I saying before about leaving my penance behind for the weekend? I'm already paying the price for deceiving the entire student body. Why should I have to pay double when I've been nothing short of the perfect angel here at home?

"Cat got your tongue?" my mother asks, raising her eyebrows. She holds out her glass. "Need some water?"

I nod gratefully, figuring the longer it takes to hack up old Fluffy, the more time I have to stall for an excuse. But Mommy Dearest seems to have lost interest in waiting.

"You drink, I'll talk," she says curtly. "And don't worry, I've got plenty to say." She glances over at my father, who gives a corroborative nod before turning to stare past me out the open window. "Glory's mother seemed to think it was a shame the alcohol and drug awareness group at your school had to disband," my mom continues, setting her agitated sights back on me. "But apparently, I should still be very proud of my daughter for becoming such a shining example of sobriety for other recovering teen addicts. I told Mrs. Finklefuss she was mistaken—that you'd never even gone away to summer camp, let alone a detox clinic—but she felt certain that you were, in fact, the president of, *and* inspiration for, this group. So, I decided to dig a little deeper." *Oh, God save us all!* Any time Mom decides to embark on an archaeological expedition, you know your ass is toast. "I logged on to the Internet to see what I could find out about this disbanded awareness group—I thought maybe there'd be a website—and what flashes across the screen no more than five minutes after I sit down?"

"A pop-up ad?" I guess lamely.

"Try an instant message from your college boyfriend upstate." *Jordan?* But we're *so* over. If we were any more dead to each other, we'd both have rigor mortis. Hmm . . . I wonder if that would be enough to get me out of this unpleasant little chat. Probably not.

"He's *not* my boyfriend," I assure her. "I don't even like him. He's a creep."

"He's my boss's son!" my dad yells, pounding his fist on the table. His glass of water nearly goes flying. *Well, that's one way to break your silence.* "The whole time you two were sneaking around like refugees, did you ever pause to remember who his father was?" *Actually, no. I guess I didn't.* He takes his gaze off the window, finally staring me straight in the eye. Now it's my turn to look away. "Did it ever occur to you that this thing you had going on with the Spelton boy might make *me* look bad?" *And the answer to that question would also be no.* I'm telling you, any time you're looking to feel like a selfish, ass-backwards piece of dung, look no farther than your own parents. They'll always be there to remind you of just how little you stop to think. About anything. Other than yourself.

"Lou," my mother cautions, trying to calm him. It's the role she assumes whenever he blows a gasket and should by no means be taken to convey that she's on my side. "Your blood pressure . . ."

My father nods, taking a deep, cleansing breath. "All I'm saying," he resumes quietly, "is what if she'd gotten pregnant?"

"We didn't even sleep together!" I protest.

"And it's a good thing," my mother says. "His girl-friend wouldn't have been too pleased." Like I said, never trust a mother with a shovel. It's ass toast every time.

"How do you know about her?" I ask.

"Jordan said he'd sent you an e-mail. When I opened it—"

"You *read* my e-mail?"

"Hey, don't give her any lip, young lady," my father warns me. "She had every right. And when you're a parent . . ." Yeah, yeah. I'd repeat what he said, but we all know how *that* speech goes.

"He wrote to thank you for not telling his sister about the two of you," my mother explains, "and to say he was sorry things didn't work out." *Translation: He's sorry he didn't get to nail a virgin.* God, what did I ever see in that skeezmeister?

"Well, it was for the best," I say. "He wasn't the right guy for me. And you both know I'm not an alcoholic. That was all just part of some giant misunderstanding that got blown way out of proportion."

"Obviously," my mom says, her worry lines beginning to show. "I think I'd remember something like shipping my teenage daughter off to dry out in *detox*. But what most concerns your father and me are all the things you've lied about."

"So, I didn't tell you about Jordan," I admit. "I'm sorry, okay? Aren't I allowed to have *some* privacy?"

"Not as long as I'm alive!" my father yells, his face turning fuschia.

"What he means is, when you're mature enough to show you can handle it," my mother clarifies. "And right now, I'd say you still have a ways to go. You didn't just lie to the kids at school or get involved in a love triangle you were worlds too naïve to be caught up in . . ." Try love *rectangle*. Or love octagon. Or . . . Who knows how many other girls Jordan was actually seeing? The *slut*. "Cindy, you nearly brought down a man's career." *Oh, boy*. Ain't no chance I'm talking my way out of *this* one. But, wait, the only way she could have found out about my showdown with Bill is if . . .

"You read my e-mails to Sammie, *too?*" I started writing her just after the shit hit the ceiling with Alona and Grace, figuring if she wouldn't take my phone calls, maybe she'd at least consider my heartfelt e-ramblings. Come to think of it, my e-mails have been more like diary entries. Good going, right? Nothing like incriminating yourself *in extensive written detail* before a full search and seizure. I swear, in the last five days, I've confessed to just about everything but the 9/11 terrorist attacks. Then again, maybe Sammie blames me for those, too. She still hasn't written me back.

"Not only did I feel I had reason enough to go through all your e-mail folders," my mother says forebodingly, "but once I learned what you'd been up to with Mr. Fenowitz, I managed to locate your secret Hotmail account. You and all these automatic logins—I swear, you made it too easy on me. I felt just like Nancy

Drew." She frowns. "I saw how you conducted yourself with this poor teacher, Cindy. Boy, you really fooled him good."

I look down at the table, suddenly so filled with shame I could choke on it. "I wasn't trying to fool him ... I thought I was in love."

"Well, what about this Jordan fellow?" my father asks. "Was that just for kicks?"

"No," I protest, looking up at them. "I mean, maybe ... I mean ..." I trail off, sighing heavily. "I don't even know anymore." And here, ladies and gentlemen, come the waterworks. "Hasn't either of you ever been young and confused?"

"Cindy, there's confused," my mother says unsympathetically, "and then there's just plain lost."

"But aren't I allowed to just be lost?" I sob. "I mean, I *am* in high school, remember?"

She raises a skeptical brow. "And yet, you're smarter than most adults I know."

"How do you figure?" I ask.

My mother shrugs. "Stealing lesson plans, setting up clandestine meetings in penthouse hotel suites ... I've met people *three times* your age who are nowhere near that calculating." *Calculating?* As in conniving, shrewd, and dishonest? My God, what an awful picture she's just painted. And of her own flesh and blood!

"It wasn't like that," I insist. "I only asked for that lesson plan so I could sound smarter during class discussion—because I wanted to impress him. It wasn't like I was using it to make cheat sheets for our next exam."

"Stealing is stealing," my mother states matter-of-factly.

"And what I'm most concerned about is this underwear party with boys," my father interjects.

"Dad, it was innocent."

"Oh, as innocent as you turned out to be?" he asks, his face becoming a bouquet of color again.

"Lou, you said you'd be calm," my mother reminds him. Then she turns to me, her left eyelid twitching like a crippled moth. This can only mean one thing: She's just as pissed as he is. But we've already covered all the bases. What could she possibly have left to slap me with? "And, let me tell you something, Cynthia Gene." Uh-oh. First *and* middle name? This might get ugly. "If you *ever* get in a car without a licensed driver again, your father and I will personally see to it that the next ride you take is straight to pedestrian hell—because you'll be walking 'til kingdom come." What on earth is she talking about? "Sammie's *intention* to get her permit one of these days doesn't make her any more qualified to drive a car than Minnie Mouse." Oh, yeah. I'd forgotten about that. But, wait, I never referred to Sammie's little vehicular infractions in those e-mails.

"How did you find out?"

"She mentioned something in her e-mail back to you today—"

"You mean Sammie wrote me back?" I exclaim, perking up a little. Okay, a lot. Is that a rainbow I see through my tears? With a big, shiny pot o' gold at the end?

"Don't interrupt your mother," my father barks. "Don't they teach manners at that fancy school of yours?"

"Sorry." Sorry, my ass! I can't believe she wrote me back! Does this mean I'm forgiven? "What did she say?" I ask tentatively.

"She just wanted to apologize for being so out of touch," my mother explains, still frowning over my bad judgment.

"And?" I press gently.

My mother sighs, clearly peeved about putting the brakes on her bitchslap in order to become my new social secretary. "She wanted to wish you a happy birthday and let you know she's no longer mad at you for telling Glory her secret. If anything, she's grateful. As for not always being honest about who you were, she said *nobody* is and not to worry—she's still your friend."

"She really said that?" I ask, becoming hopeful that with Sammie's forgiveness, I just might find it permissible to one day forgive myself.

"I think the line was, 'There's no way you could possibly be any faker than my tan.'"

I start to laugh, but my mother's stern glare snuffs out all my chuckles.

"You know, I wasn't too amused, Cindy. I'm glad you made up with your friend and that she's getting help for her illness, but she's got another thing coming if she thinks she can take *my* kid out joyriding without a license. She said when she gets back, you can both go for your permits together and will no longer have to risk cruising around illegally in her BMW." My mom pauses to shake her head. "Are these the kinds of values you were raised with?"

"No," I say. "And Sammie's not a rotten person, either. It's just that . . ." *How can I explain this?* "Good kids do bad things all the time. It's how we learn." *And sometimes we just want to have a little fun.* "If you guys think I've changed just because of a few lousy decisions I've made since we moved, then that makes me really sad." I see my mother's eyes softening and decide to lay it on a little thicker. I mean, if they pity me, they can't punish me, right? Besides, what would be the point? I already feel bad enough, and it's not as if I haven't learned my lesson. "No matter how much I might screw up, I never thought either of you would question my character. I always took for granted that you two would be able to see past my mistakes, straight through to the real me, that *you'd both* always know exactly who I was—even when I wasn't so sure."

"Oh, baby," my mom gushes, her eyes filling up, "of course we know the real you." *Jackpot.*

My father turns to me, flashing a wry, halfhearted smile. "We also know you're going to be grounded for the rest of your natural-born life."

# twenty-six making wishes

*Happy birthday to you*
*Happy birthday to you*
*You are a pathetic retard*
*And you smell like one, too . . .*

So, how much does this bite? My sixteenth birthday and
I'm spending it at home—alone in my room, in a pair
of dirty old sweats, listening to Janis sing the blues.
Alex hasn't even called me yet. No sweet, slobbery
e-card either. To be fair, I should mention that I never
told him today was my big day. I guess you can say I was
testing him to see if he'd remember on his own. *Note to
self: Never give a boy a test you're not one hundred percent
positive he's going to pass. Unless, of course, you're a glutton for
punishment (which would definitely have to be the case for me,*

*considering I'm* already *punished . . . and on my* birthday, *no less . . . Have I mentioned how much this blows?).*

Grounded or not, I suppose I'll still get a cake later. So, at least I can look forward to drowning my sorrows in a big, buttery hunk of frosted fat. Of course, first I'll have to make my ceremonial birthday wish and huff out those sixteen candles. But what'll I wish for? I guess if wax, wicks, and fire had the power to turn back time, I'd have those pretty little candles fix it so that we'd never even moved here. No, wait . . . that's not a good one. Because then I wouldn't have ever met Sammie. Or Glory, who was worth knowing while it lasted, even though she still avoids me like a flaming sack of shit every day on the school bus. I guess if I had one wish, one birthday wish that might come true, it would be for Alex to finally kiss me. To take me in his arms and plant a wet one on my lips that would erase the scars of my stupidity— of Jordan, Bill, and the last three months—and show me how he really feels. Yeah, *right.* Who am I kidding? Birthday wishes never come true. Especially not for retarded, inexperienced virgins who lie about being sexually skilled alcoholics just to win a few extra chums.

It's 4:47 p.m., and still no word from Alex. I could at least *shower*—get out of these crusty old duds—but what's the point when I'm only gonna get dirty again tomorrow? When there's no one to see and nothing to do? I know my parents were right to ground me. They'd have been right if I'd only committed *one* of the crimes they busted me for. But knowing they were right, having "learned something from all this"—that in the end, all lying buys you is false friends—doesn't make being punished any easier. It still sucks big, hairy antelope balls. Can you blame me for not exactly being in a festive mood?

"Cindy?" my mother says suddenly, shaking me from my trance. How long has she been standing there? "Sorry to startle you, but you have a visitor."

"Hey, stranger," says the voice. The familiar, home-grown, softspoken voice of the one person who knows me better than I know myself . . . and likes me anyway. "Happy birthday."

"Alex!" I exclaim, jumping to my feet. "You remembered!"

"I'll leave you two alone," my mother says, heading for the door.

"You mean, you actually trust me to be alone up here with a boy?" I ask. "After all that's happened?"

"I trust Alex," she fires back with a little wink. "It's wonderful to see you again, honey," she tells him. And with that, she makes her exit.

"It *is* wonderful to see you," I say, sizing him up, from his close-cropped haircut and POP MUSIC SUX T-shirt to his trademark baggy jeans and black sneakers. And, of course, Alex wouldn't be Alex without his favorite green hoodie, unzipped and oversized as ever. Okay, so I guess you all finally see where I got my fashion sense. Or lack thereof. Actually, Alex and I sort of grew into the no-style style together. He nearly died laughing when I told him we'd inspired a revolution in suburbia. "You look great."

He laughs. I love his laugh. It feels like . . . home. "I look exactly the same. You know, I don't think I've washed this jacket since the last time I saw you."

"Now, *that's* rebel chic."

He laughs again. "*You* look amazing, though. Very mature, very sixteen."

"Really?" I ask, glancing into the mirror. *Oh, holy fuckdust! Why didn't any of you tell me I look like toilet mold?* That's the problem with being in love with your best friend. You're so used to feeling comfortable, you forget to worry about the little things—like hair and makeup and not smelling like a dead foot. "Oh, God, don't look at me!" I yelp, ducking down. "I'm hideous! If I'd known you were coming—"

"It wouldn't have been a surprise," he says, hugging me. *Whoa, Nellie. I think I'm melting . . . melting . . .* "So, I noticed your development has a basketball court. You up for a little one-on-one?"

"I thought you'd never ask."

★ ★ ★

In honor of Alex's first official visit to Beaubridge, the wardens gave me special permission to leave the grounds. And here I stand, ready to reclaim my title in a match that's been ongoing since I was still a brace-faced midget waiting for my first period to come along and ruin my life. Actually, I've only beaten Alex once—back in 2005 when his left arm was in a sling—and I've never felt less competitive than I do today. But I can't say I mind the idea of seeing him sweat.

"Ready to lose?" I ask, dribbling the ball as we set foot onto the court.

"Oh *yeah*," he teases, swiping the ball out from under me. "I'm shaking." He shoots. He scores. "Play 'til twenty-one?"

"Hey, the rules haven't changed just because it's been a while."

Alex tosses me the ball. "Then, show me what you've got, Ace."

*Twelve overwhelmingly unsuccessful minutes later . . .*

"So, what are we up to now?" Alex asks, squinting up

at the basket as the ball swishes through the net. (His shot, of course.) "Nine hundred–nothing?"

I put my hands on my hips, glaring at him. "Ha ha."

"Oh, my bad. *Twenty*–nothing," he says as the ball bounces between us.

I lunge forward, grabbing hold of it. "You know, just because you're beating me doesn't mean you're better."

"What's it mean, then?" he asks, slipping out of his hoodie, which he tosses behind him onto the blacktop. He begins waving his arms in front of my face, playfully trying to psyche me out. "What's the matter, birthday girl? Can't take the heat?" This is when I notice it—the beat-up old bracelet on his right wrist.

"Oh my God! You still wear that?" I say, completely dropping the ball as I grab his hand for a closer look. "I never took mine off, either. See?"

For a moment, Alex seems embarrassed and, for the first time since he got here, I can see the hurt on his face, the pain that I caused when I turned my back on our friendship. But it isn't long before his sadness becomes a smile—we both know the past is behind us and today is a brand-new beginning.

"You know you'll never go pro with that playing style," he teases. "You think Michael Jordan ever just stopped dribbling in the middle of a game to hold hands with Magic Johnson?"

The boy does have a point there. Laughing, I let go of him and turn to see where the ball has bobbled off to.

"Hey, wait a second," Alex says, putting his arms around my waist. He pulls me closer. "I didn't say I didn't like it." Okay, *this* is new. Alex has never made a move on me. *Ever.* Even the day he asked me to be his girlfriend, we were sitting at least a foot apart on the cold cement steps outside his parents' house and had just finished having a contest to see who could make the longest Mountain Dew burp. (P.S. I won.) This feels different. Older. Sexier. Right.

"Well, you should say what you like more often," I tell him.

"Oh yeah?" He smiles, his hypnotic green eyes twinkling in a way I've never seen before.

"What are you thinking?" I ask.

"I'm thinking I might like to kiss you." Oh, sweet mother of me . . . The boy is *serious!*

I wrap my arms around his neck, my whole body tingling in anticipation of a moment I've been waiting for since I was twelve. "Go for it."

Well, what do you know? I guess sometimes birthday wishes really *do* come true.

# twenty-seven the truth about high school

Glory Finklefuss once told me she didn't mind being treated like an embarrassing fungal ass rash I refused to let the Four Tops find out about, explaining that she was content to stick to her kind and let me party with mine "because you know what, hey, that's high school." Funny how even with her farmer threads and glow-in-the-dark afro, Glory still knew it was *all* about appearances.

But she was wrong. I mean, she was wrong to put up with that sort of treatment. I was a creep for dishing it out. I realize now that I never deserved her. Would you totally crap your Calvins if I told you she was actually speaking to me again?

We started talking a couple of months ago after the *Beat* ran a revealing exposé on the former president of DAAG, telling the whole school they'd never had an alcoholic leader. Apparently, "somebody" leaked the story of my clean and sober past to Kara Fargus, who agreed to pull her piece on a certain sophomore battling bulimia at a clinic out west in exchange for an exclusive interview with yours truly. Back at my old school, on the "mean streets" of Philadelphia, the student newspaper would've never gotten away with gossip-rag journalism like Kara's, but the powers that be at Beaubridge seem to have taken a hands-off approach to the amateur press, which is great for our ruthless editor, who thrives on tabloid tell-alls like the piece I let her write on me. I figured the truth would piss a lot of people off, but what did I care? No one was talking to me anyway. Turns out some people actually admire honesty—through Kara's sleazeball article, I was able to reach the one person who really mattered.

"Hey," Glory said as I hopped off the school bus that afternoon. "I read your interview, and . . . Wow, that took a lot of guts," she concluded with a nervous giggle. "After all that's happened—all the lying and covering up—I wasn't too sure you had any."

"I don't," I admitted sadly. "I just didn't want people looking up to me for no reason, thinking I'd overcome something huge, when I've never overcome anything in my life."

"Ah, that's not true," she said, shoving me playfully. "You overcame Alona and Grace."

"Same way you overcame me?"

Glory shook her head, the warm breeze whispering through her kooky carrot-colored locks. "I never got over you, CG. I just needed some time. You *really* hurt me—more than I could ever explain. But I've been talking with Samara, and if I can forgive her," she said, a slow grin spreading across her face, "I guess I can forgive you, too." That's when I realized the big man upstairs had officially crossed me off his shit list.

"Oh, thank you, thank you!" I gushed, hugging her like some shameless game show contestant who'd just won the big money prize. "I'm so happy! I've missed you like crazy, Glory."

"Yeah," she said with a satisfied smile. "I guess I've missed you, too."

"And just to prove to you how much I've changed, I'll tell you why else I gave Kara Fargus that interview, aside from merely wanting to come clean."

"To promote your upcoming spread in *Hustler*?" she teased.

"No, that won't be out until Christmas."

Glory shook her head, laughing. "You always were too quick for me."

"Well, quick wit comes in handy, especially when you're dealing with opportunistic snakes like Kara."

"Do tell," she insisted, her big brown eyes brimming with curiosity.

"Well, it seems she had gotten her hands on Sammie's records and was planning an in-depth segment on eating disorders for this week's issue *until* I floated a better story her way. Of course, this was only in exchange for her solemn vow that she'd never print a single word about our favorite recovering bulimic."

Glory was impressed. "Well, *somebody's* savvy! And you definitely win Friend of the Year for martyring yourself like that to save Samara." She looked at me doubtfully.

"But?"

"But how do you know Kara won't still print the bulimia story now that she's gotten your interview?"

"Because she could get kicked out of school for snooping in Sammie's files. I overheard her confessing the entire crime to one of her writers in the bathroom while I was eating lunch the other day. I mean, I know the faculty believes in freedom of the press, but not by *any* means necessary—especially when those means involve violating school property. God, who knew high school journalism could be so riddled with danger and espionage?"

"Wait a minute. You were eating lunch in the *bath-*

room?" Glory exclaimed, changing the subject, her jaw gaping open in shock. "What *for?*"

"I don't know ..." I fumbled as the heat rushed to my face. Until that point, I'd done a pretty good job of hiding my shitter-side status at school, and although it was only Glory, I somehow felt as if I'd just been caught with my pants down for the whole world to see. Like I was experiencing some kind of global wardrobe malfunction even Janet Jackson would've snickered about We're talking *total* humiliation.

"Oh my God," Glory said, covering her mouth. "I just realized that with Grace and Alona out of the picture, you've been roaming the halls all this time without a single friend to your name!" *And that ego lift was brought to you by ...* "What happened between you guys, anyway?"

"It's a long story," I told her. "But in case I haven't said it enough, I really *am* sorry for everything that happened between you and me. Our friendship was a bazillion times more special than what I had with Alona and Grace. It's not as if I can just turn around and villify them as the most evil, plastic überwhores who ever walked the planet, but I do know they weren't the right friends for me. I guess deep down, I always knew that. You, on the other hand ... I was more honest with you than anybody, and still," I said, sighing remorsefully, "I lied about so much." I knew that if Glory and I were really going to start over, it had to be from someplace truly honest. As honest as an exposed fungal ass rash. "Jordan Spelton was never really my boyfriend," I confessed. "I mean, we were seeing each other, but never as seriously as I made it sound. At least, *he* wasn't serious."

"Well, thank God for small favors," she said. "From what I've heard, he's not exactly the best catch on dry land."

"You mean, from what *Grace* has told you?" I asked, raising my eyebrows.

Glory looked away, shrugging her shoulders.

"It's okay. You don't need to keep her secret anymore. I *know*. She told me. The question is, why'd you leave the cat in the bag for so long? All this time, you've had the power to destroy Grace—God knows she's tried to destroy you—but instead you've been protecting her. I don't get it."

"We were so close for so long," she said plainly. "I kept hoping this whole popularity thing might just be a phase, and I guess in the back of my mind I never wanted to do anything to spoil the chances of . . ." Glory trailed off, frowning wistfully.

"Grace one day coming to her senses and realizing what an incredible friend she lost by letting you go?"

"Something like that," Glory admitted. "Pathetic, huh?"

"No, you just give her way too much credit, that's all. Grace is nowhere near as smart as she seems. I thought she had a brain in there somewhere, but she let me down. As far as I can see, she's always gonna be *somebody's* puppet, whether the one pulling the strings happens to be Jordan or Alona or some other unlucky schmuck she's only using to fill the hole inside her soul. And she'll never stop exploiting that emptiness as her excuse to be a first-class bitch."

Glory nodded knowingly. "Her famous mean streak— it's how she's always dealt with her insecurities."

"Not to mention her frustrations," I added. "And her pain."

"Ah, she's a pain in my *ass,*" Glory concluded with a dismissive wave of her hand. "I'm surprised she hasn't given us both hemorrhoids by now."

"Yeah," I said, laughing. "Who needs her? Actually, come to think of it, I guess Alona does, or else *she'd* be the one with no friends. Imagine that."

"It would never happen," Glory said, shaking her bright, woolly mane. "Before Grace could even get one foot out the door, there'd be thousands lining up to steal her shoes. Actually, I heard they're already auditioning for *your* replacement. If that's how popularity works, I guess I really *was* cut out to be a nerd. I could never understand why Samara and Grace always put so much stock into what other people thought of them."

"Everyone cares to some extent," I had to remind her. "Well, everyone except for you. You know, Glory, when it comes down to it, you might just be the biggest rebel of all."

"And don't you ever forget it," she said, smiling broadly.

"Hey, speaking of Sammie, whose side do you think she'll end up taking—in public, anyway?" I asked.

"Hmm, that's a real toss-up," Glory teased. "Who will the chronically image-obsessed Samara choose to side with—debutante prom queens Blondie and Bitchie, who come complete with built-in status protection, or their exiled archrival Toilet Girl and her barely known partner-in-crime Farmer Frizzyfuss?"

I couldn't help but laugh. "Yeah, I guess it's a no-brainer. But we'll see for sure when she gets back next week."

"Until then," Glory said, reaching out to shake my hand. "Allow me to welcome you to Nerdsburg, where I have spent the last two years living and working as a social misfit. Of course, this humble community may pale in comparison with the wild times you enjoyed in the fast lane, but overall, I think you'll find that being a certified loser isn't nearly as bad as it's cracked up to be.

After all, there are more of us than there are of them, which leads me to wonder how *we* ever came to be regarded as the odd ones out in the first place. But in any event, I do hope you'll enjoy your stay."

"You know, I get the feeling you've been living in Nerdsburg a lot longer than two years," I told her. "But that's cool. I'm looking forward to being misfit losers with you."

And guess who ended up joining us? Turns out Sammie's image obsession wasn't quite as chronic as we thought—she doesn't mind being seen around the halls with Farmer Frizzyfuss and Toilet Girl after all. Rehab really worked wonders on her psyche. Aside from getting a handle on her weight wars, she's actually learned to like herself again. Maybe even for the first time ever. The new and improved Sammie is confident, vivacious . . . less orange. She's excited to wake up and face each new day in Nerdsburg with her two best friends by her side and couldn't give a rat's nut what other people think of her anymore, least of all Alona and Grace, who have gone ahead and adopted a brand-new pair of blow-up dolls to be their ladies in waiting for next year.

Yes, school is officially out for summer. Today was the last day, *thank God*. Not that it wasn't all worth it— getting punched in the nose, having my heart broken by the devil's only son, being grounded on my sixteenth birthday. Because without those miserable bumps lining the road, I'd have never found my path to happiness—a path lined with true friends, real trust, and a lot of good, old-fashioned *me*. Sounds cheesy as a ten-pound wheel of cheddar, I know, but the truth is, the light at the end of the tunnel was waiting for me all along. I just had to plow through a minefield full of donkey shit to get there. And it wasn't all bad. In some ways, plowing through that donkey dung was the most fun I've ever had. But I'm still glad to have made it to the other side. And to have actually lived to tell about it.

You know, I once thought moving to Beaubridge was my big chance to finally *be* somebody. But since then I've realized something—it's tough enough just being myself. Without all the extra frosting and fireworks. And that even straight-up à la carte, I'm still "somebody" enough for me. Right now, I guess you could say I'm working on being the best me I can be. God knows, I screw up a lot, but the good news is it's a role I know I've got plenty of years to grow into. It may not be a spine-tingling persona like my daredevil alter ego's, but at least it's authentic. And the way I see it, no matter how imperfect I might be, nobody—despite their hardest efforts—can play the part of Cindy Gene Silverman better than I can. Glory and Sammie still call me CG, but at least they know who I am now. Even more importantly, *I* know who I am.

That day at the Speltons' anniversary party—the day the shit hit the fan, knocked me out, and left me stinking for dead—Alona asked who I really was. I've had lots of time to think about her question since then, and the truth is I'm just a simple kid from Philly. A kid who'd rather shoot hoops than go shopping. A kid who knows every lyric to every Led Zeppelin song ever recorded but wouldn't know the Jonas Brothers from a crack in her own ass. Someone who knows it's not about money or possessions or the name on the sole of her shoes. A girl who's happiest just kicking around in comfortable clothes with comfortable friends, without worrying about status or image—just playing the part of herself.

I've come to accept that high school is all about playing parts, living up to or raging against our labels. And trust me, it's even more about labels—the geeks, the snobs, the jocks. And within each crowd are *more* labels—the smart one, the pretty one, the rebel. But you really can't judge a book by its cover. Whoever thought Mr. Fenowitz would turn out to be such a colossal bore? Or Jordan, so rotten? Sammie, so strong? And Grace, so weak? Whoever thought popularity could be so complicated and yet, at the same time, so monumentally meaningless? Shit if I know. My brain is still fried from finals, and about the only thing I do know is that I'm ready to ditch all the backbiting, shitslinging, stereotyping bull-doody that is high school for a nice, long summer vaca-tion with my boyfriend.

Yup, Alex finally popped the big question (again), and this time I said yes. We haven't been able to venture anywhere more exotic than this butt pimple of a suburb they call Beaubridge, considering I'm still grounded 'til my funeral, but it doesn't matter—I'm happier than a pig in proverbial caca just being with him at all. To have made it through these last five months without com-pletely losing my sanity. And on top of everything, have found love. To still have Glory and Sammie. To still have me.

So, I wasn't a rebel after all. And when it comes down to it, I had fifteen minutes of fame. A flash in the pan of popularity. No one will even remember my name next year, let alone care that I was once friends with the forever-fabulous Alona Spelton. But don't worry—I'll be just fine. Because you know what, hey, that's high school.

# Acknowledgments

I am beyond grateful to my agent, Susan Schulman, for taking a chance on me, believing in my work, and leading this book to Karen Grove, whose thoughtful insights helped turn it into so much more than I ever knew it could be. I must also thank my ever-supportive and enthusiastic parents for sharing in every pitfall and triumph this business has to offer and always believing I'd make it (again). And last but not least, there is my long-suffering husband, Scott, without whom few things are possible.

Thank you all for helping me realize this dream. I am truly blessed.